GHOSTS OF BERLIN

STORIES

GHOSTS
OF
BERLIN

STORIES

RUDOLPH HERZOG

TRANSLATED BY EMMA RAULT

MELVILLE HOUSE
BROOKLYN · LONDON

Ghosts of Berlin: Stories

First published as *Truggestalten* in 2017 by Galiani Berlin
Copyright © 2017 Verlag Kiepenheuer & Witsch, Koln
Translation copyright © 2019 by Melville House Publishing
All rights reserved
First Melville House Printing: October 2019

Melville House Publishing   Suite 2000
            46 John Street   and   16/18 Woodford Road
        Brooklyn, NY 11201   London E7 oHA

mhpbooks.com
@melvillehouse

ISBN: 978-1-61219-751-7
ISBN: 978-1-61219-752-4 (ebook)

Designed by Beste M. Dogan

Printed in the United States of America

1 3 5 7 9 10 8 6 4 2

A catalog record for this book is available from the Library of Congress
Library of Congress Control Number: 2019945916

GHOSTS OF BERLIN

TANDEM

WHEN HE WAS THIRTEEN, DIMITRI had his first asthma attack. He was playing basketball in the school gym when all of a sudden he felt his windpipe contract, as if from the size of a firehose to the circumference of a straw. A doctor was quickly called to treat him, but the high dosage of cortisone pills he prescribed made Dimitri's face swell up. The attacks became a regular occurrence—a smoke-filled *kafenio* or a swim in the sea could cause a bout so vicious that his friends would have to come to his aid and rush him home.

Dimitri's grandmother was convinced that the water was to blame for his condition. She insisted that the family buy an eel for the well. "It'll eat up the muck in there." At first, his parents ignored her advice, but after he had several attacks in quick succession, Dimitri's mother gave in. When he pulled aside the heavy slab that covered the mouth of the well, he'd see it down there—a long, thin shadow, swimming in slow circles at the bottom.

Though their cottage in the Pindos mountains now had cleaner water, Dimitri's asthma didn't get any better. One morning, Dimitri found the eel floating dead on the surface, and his father had to fish it out before it could contaminate the water supply. Dimitri's mother, fed up with pills and remedies, finally made an appointment for him with a city doctor.

The doctor gave him two inhalers—a blue one for daily doses, and an extra-powerful red one for emergencies. For many years, Dimitri never left home without stuffing both of them into the pockets of his jeans.

Time passed, and Dimitri grew into an affable, if rather over-cautious young man. He did quite well in school, and was accepted to the prestigious Athens University of Economics and Business. There he discovered that he not only had a knack for trade, but also an aptitude for languages. He was hired right out of college by the Athens office of an international industrial conglomerate based in Munich. Dimitri would often fly there for meetings, sometimes giving himself a few hours to explore the city or have a drink with his German colleagues afterward before catching a flight home. Though he rarely needed it now, he still stored the emergency inhaler in his briefcase so he'd always know where it was.

When the economic crisis got hold of Greece and wouldn't let go, Dimitri's cushy life came to an abrupt end. He received notification from his German employers that they were shutting down their operations in Greece, and that his position was to be terminated.

Some months later, when one of Dimitri's former colleagues got in touch to check up on him, Dimitri confessed that he was making ends meet by managing a souvlaki shop. His colleague had moved to Berlin and suggested that his employment prospects would be better there, but Dimitri wasn't so sure. Though he had a bit of money saved up to tide him over while he looked for a job, he was worried about his German. While it was good enough to get by in everyday life, he felt it was in no way adequate for conducting business meetings or negotiating deals. But his colleague insisted. He was about to leave for a sabbatical, and Dimitri was welcome to stay at his place while he was away. It would be a better investment to bone up on his German, his colleague said, than to pay rent.

✖

Dimitri arrived to a city alight with an autumnal palette of browns and golds. They reminded him of the intense colors that swept across the mountains of his childhood home around this time of year. With every gust of wind, leaves blew down from the trees in shimmering cascades. A few tumbled onto the windshield of Dimitri's taxi as it made its way to the north Berlin neighborhood of Prenzlauer Berg. In front of the building where it dropped him off, a man was slowly progressing down the sidewalk with a leaf blower. He blasted a jet of air into the gutter, whirling serrated chestnut leaves all about the ground. A second man followed close behind, raking up the leaves and shoveling them into a bright-or-ange trash bag. The men paused to let Dimitri pass as he dragged his suitcase up to the marble entrance, fished the keys his colleague had sent him from his bag, and let himself in.

The apartment was a spacious studio. His friend had partitioned the room with the clever use of bookshelves and Japanese screens. Dimitri was anxious to get started on his plans. Even before unpack-ing, he had connected to the Wi-Fi and was on his laptop looking up classes. There was a language school that took rolling admissions within walking distance of the apartment. He could start the next day. Without a second thought, he paid for a two-month course.

This turned out to be a mistake. Though he had selected the intermediary level, the exercises were annoyingly basic—just con-versations about the weather and food. After three days Dimitri's patience ran out, and he asked for his money back.

The experience had discouraged him from enrolling in another school, so the day after he dropped out, Dimitri set off to wander around the neighborhood and plan his next move. He knew little about Prenzlauer Berg save that it had once been a popular spot for artists and bohemians, though everything around him seemed more expensive than any genuine bohemian could afford. On Pappelallee, a bustling thoroughfare, every other storefront appeared to house some chic café or boutique. BMWs and Mercedes-Benzes lined the street.

Dimitri found himself walking through a small park where young mothers and nannies sat on benches gently rocking the strollers in front of them. He noticed a cluster of weatherworn tombstones, which seemed out of place in a public park. At the far end, there was a nondescript building with the words *Bibliothek am Friedhof* emblazoned on its windows. The Cemetery Library? Was he reading that right? Curious now, he entered the building. Despite its name, the library's interior was unremarkable. Two large halls full of books flanked the entrance, with computer terminals clustered in the middle. There appeared to be more visitors browsing the web than the shelves. It seemed like your run-of-the-mill library, right down to the silence that was policed by a stocky middle-aged woman just waiting for someone to violate the rules.

"Can I help you?"

Dimitri cast a quick glance around the room before turning his attention to her.

"Yes, I hope so," Dimitri said. "I'm looking to improve my German."

"Well, we don't offer language classes," said the woman flatly.

"I'm not looking for classes. I am not that bad of a German speaker. I just want to polish it a bit."

"I see," she said. "We have language books and audio that you can check out, if you like."

Dimitri envisioned himself sitting alone in his apartment listening to language lessons on his headphones. It was a depressing prospect.

"No, I don't think that will do for me. Are there any other options? Some sort of study group?"

She looked at him over her glasses. Dimitri sensed that her patience was running thin.

"Well, what languages *are* you fluent in? English?"

"Sure. But my first language is Greek."

"Then perhaps you can post a classified ad online for a tandem partner."

"I'm sorry, I don't know what that is."

"It's a type of language exchange. You meet up with someone who wants to learn Greek. You speak German; they reply in Greek. You correct one another as you go along. Is there anything else I can help you with?"

She looked at Dimitri expectantly.

"Those tombstones just outside. Are they real?"

"Of course they're real."

"It's weird them just being in the middle of the park, isn't it?"

"I guess. It used to be the Atheists' Cemetery, if you want to look it up." She gestured toward the shelves at the far end of the room.

With that, the librarian grabbed a handful of books from the returns pile and began typing away at the keyboard in front of her. She paused and gave Dimitri one final, resolute look.

"If you end up doing your studying here in the main library, please remember to turn off your phone and keep quiet. Danke!"

Late that night, Dimitri googled various groups for people looking for language partners, but no one seemed interested in learning Greek as a trade-off. Finally, he ended up on a message board for Berlin-based travelers. The site was entirely text-based. No images or animated GIFs, just messages requesting and offering all sorts of things: used armchairs, sex, exotic pets. He timidly typed in a simple message in English:

Greek seeking German for tandem language exchange over coffee. Please inquire Dimitri Papadopoulos.

He entered his email address and hit send. He briefly wondered if he had been too vague in his post, but resisted the urge to return to it. As Dimitri prepared for bed, he could feel his despair growing. He tried to shake it off by scrolling through news articles. The reports of the worsening crisis in Greece weren't helping to give him peace of mind. He put aside his phone and lay there in the dark, trying to relax.

He was startled awake by the sound of an email arriving in his inbox. He grabbed his phone instinctively, squinting at the glare of the screen. It was from a stranger, a woman.

Dear Mr. Papadopoulos:

Many thanks for your message. I have been looking for someone to help me improve my knowledge of your beautiful language, and I would likewise be delighted to help you with your German. I only have free time later in the evenings, however, so I'm afraid meeting for coffee won't be possible. If that's not an issue for you, would you consider having dinner with me on Thursday at the Bateau Ivre on Heinrichplatz?

My best,
Lotte Wuttcke

Dimitri quickly wrote back asking if she could specify a time, to which Lotte replied with reciprocal speed:

How about 10:00 p.m.? I'll put a white aster on the table so you'll be able to recognize me. —LW

Dimitri checked the dictionary to verify that an aster was a flower. Then he replied to confirm the appointment.

✖

That Thursday evening, a thunderstorm swept through the streets of Berlin. Dimitri held on tightly to his large beige umbrella as he ran from his front door to the bus stop two blocks away. By the time he got there, his leather loafers were soaked through with rainwater. Mercifully, the M29 bus pulled up at the little glass shelter only minutes later. He stamped his pass and sat down in the front row of the lower deck. The bus shot off, careening through the downpour at breakneck speed. A barrage of fat raindrops pelted against the dark windows, and though Dimitri could only dimly make out the street, he noticed the high beams of cars swerving to avoid the bus. Dimitri glanced out at the street again and realized the driver was steering the vehicle right down the middle of the road. A woman walked up to the front of the bus to complain about his reckless driving, but he ignored her. He was sitting hunched over, his hands clutching the wheel, like a coachman gripping his reins. When the woman kept up her protestations, the driver turned his head away from the road to glare at her. There were heavy bags under his eyes, the kind you tend to see in long-time drinkers.

Although he didn't look especially angry, the complainant immediately fell silent and slunk back to her seat. Soon afterward, she pressed the green button, which let out a loud bleep.

The bus pulled over immediately. "Heinrichplatz," a disembodied female voice intoned over the speaker. Dimitri picked up his umbrella. The door opened with a hiss and both Dimitri and the woman stepped out, heading off in opposite directions.

✖

The rain had fogged up the windows of the restaurant. Inside, heads were bobbing to and fro as if suspended on long threads. While the guests were engrossed in conversation, a waiter made the rounds of the packed tables with a tray balanced on his hand. He too was reduced to a blurry shadow. Dimitri stepped through the door into the restaurant's muggy clamor. Now he could clearly see the diners. He scanned the room for the white aster, spotting a flower with a ray of creamy petals on the table in the far corner of the room. Seated there was a delicate yet dignified woman with white-blonde shoulder-length hair. Her skin, too, was pale, almost translucent. He guessed her to be around his age, in her late thirties, early forties. He caught her eye and waved, making his way toward her.

"Frau Wuttcke?"

She smiled at him, revealing a fine mesh of wrinkles that made Dimitri begin to second-guess her age.

"You don't have to be so formal, Dimitri," she said in German-tinged Greek. "Lotte is fine." She rose to greet him and gently shook his hand. It felt cool. She surveyed him, flashing a smile.

"You don't look the way I imagined you," she said.

"How so?" he replied in German, sitting down across from her. He was thinking the same about her.

"I imagined you would have a darker complexion."

"That's just a stereotype," replied Dimitri. "There are Greeks who could pass as Northern Europeans. We come in many varieties."

"Hmm. German men only come in two types, unfortunately."

"Oh?" Dimitri asked. "And what are those?"

"Barbarians and bureaucrats," she said with a wry laugh. "Not much of a choice."

Her amusement had a contagious effect on Dimitri, who caught himself chuckling along with her.

"It's a little peculiar to be here having a conference with a strange man like this."

"I think you mean *synantó*—meeting someone—not *synedriázo*—which means having a meeting or conference."

"Of course, how silly of me," she said, slapping her forehead lightly.

"But otherwise, your Greek is very good."

"Thank you," Lotte replied. "So is your German."

There was a momentary silence between them. Lotte took another sip of her wine, keeping her eyes firmly trained on Dimitri all the while. He breathed a sigh of relief when the waiter appeared. Lotte quickly snatched up a menu.

"You go ahead, Dimitri."

"I'll have the spätzle," he said, gesturing for Lotte to order too.

"Could I have the steak?"

"And how would you like it?" asked the waiter, scribbling on his notepad.

"Could you serve it *bleu*?"

"We could, yes, but it will be cold inside. Is that okay?"

"That's perfect," said Lotte.

"What is bleu steak?" Dimitri asked.

"It's raw steak," she explained, "like tartare, but with a seared coating. It was my husband who introduced me to this dish. He always liked to order it."

"Is he . . ."

"Deceased? Yes."

"I'm sorry to hear that."

Dimitri gave Lotte a sympathetic look.

"It was many years ago. It makes me happy to speak about him. If that doesn't bother you."

"Of course not," said Dimitri tentatively. "Tell me about him."

"Well, he was actually the one who got me interested in Greece. You see, he was an archaeologist and spent a lot of time there working on excavation sites. I often accompanied him."

"Really? Whereabouts?"

"He spent most of his time around Ioannina," replied Lotte. "Beautiful city. Have you been?"

"Yes, actually, I'm from the Pindos region."

"Such stunning mountains. We never got a chance to explore them, but you could see them from the house where we stayed. The lake too. What's it called again?"

"Lake Pamvotida."

"Right! I remember now." Lotte nodded thoughtfully. "My husband worked on the Dodoni amphitheater site, not too far from town. I liked to stay behind and explore the shops across from the old castle walls. It was as if the place had been left untouched by the last century."

Dimitri wasn't sure what Lotte meant. During World War Two, Ioannina had been brutalized by the German occupying forces. There were monuments all over town in remembrance of these atrocities.

"It is peaceful there today," said Dimitri, "but during the war, Ioannina and several of the towns surrounding it were . . ."

Was he crossing a line? How did Germans feel when the war was brought up? He hesitated, wondering whether he would offend Lotte.

". . . devastated by the German army."

Lotte nodded and lowered her eyes to the table.

"I hope you don't mind me saying this."

"It's alright," she said after a moment. "I know about it. The bombing raids, the massacres, the deportations. I meant that it is astonishing that the city should have recovered." She paused. "In that way Ioannina is a bit like Berlin, where the remnants of history have even become tourist attractions. It's incredible, considering the bleak past. I find that so interesting. My husband, on the other hand, wouldn't have thought so. He preferred to focus on the battles of antiquity. Anything to do with the war wasn't his thing."

Lotte went quiet again. Dimitri wondered whether he had offended her after all, or if it was talking about her husband that was upsetting her. He took a slow sip of his water to give her a few seconds to gather herself.

"Lotte, are you okay?"

She raised her head and nodded at him, picking up on his unease.

"Well, now you know something about me. What about you?"

Now it was Dimitri's turn to share a little bit about himself. He gave her a brief version of his life story, right up to losing his job and deciding to start fresh in Berlin. He also touched on Greece's economic upheaval, with Lotte correcting his German at various points along the way. He was so absorbed in trying to put his thoughts into German that he didn't at first notice Lotte's leg lightly touching his.

"Such a shame you had to leave Greece," she said, looking into his eyes. "It's such a beautiful country, especially the people."

"Yes," he replied nervously. "It is a beautiful country. Just like Germany." Only when he stopped speaking did he discover that she had not taken her leg away.

He felt his breath tighten.

"Will you excuse me?"

Dimitri got up and went to find the bathroom. He turned on the tap, cupped his hands, and splashed his face with cold water, taking a moment to regain his composure. After a few deep breaths he returned to the table to find that their food had come.

"This looks delicious," he said, doing his best to sound casual. He quickly unwrapped his cutlery and started on his meal. Lotte sliced into her steak, which was garnished with fresh horseradish. She seemed very engrossed in the activity, wielding her knife with taut precision.

"You're very hungry," Dimitri said.

She looked up from her plate and straight at him. There was something resolute in her glance, as if her true nature was only now revealing itself. Her pupils were unusually small, her irises a piercing blue. For a moment, a thin layer of frost settled over their conversation. Phil Collins was burbling in the background, the nineties stuck in an endless loop. Lotte carefully put down her silverware. Her expression softened.

"I'm sorry—I sometimes lose myself when I eat. Probably not the best habit in a language partner."

Immediately after they'd finished their meal, Lotte called over the waiter with an elegant gesture and asked for the bill. Taken aback by the abrupt end to their meeting, Dimitri handed the waiter his card. Lotte tried to protest, but finally relented. Then her face suddenly brightened.

"I've just remembered. I have something for you."

She pulled out a package wrapped in oilcloth.

"I like to bake bread," she said, somewhat sheepishly. "It's one of my hobbies. But I always bake more than I can eat. So I thought you might like a loaf."

She handed the bundle to Dimitri, who gave it a squeeze. It felt dense and heavy.

"What kind of bread is this?"

"It's my special recipe. I won't give away its ingredients, but maybe you can tell me what you think at our next *synántisi*?"

Lotte pulled out a leather-bound calendar book from her purse.

"Let's say the same time and place tomorrow."

She hadn't presented it as a question, and without much thought Dimitri agreed.

It was just past midnight by the time he got home. The rain had stopped, and the streets were quiet outside his bedroom window. He lay in bed thinking about Lotte. Aside from what she had told him about her husband, Lotte hadn't really shared anything about herself. It bothered him that he had failed to ask her more; he was usually very considerate about such things. And he was genuinely curious about her life.

Unable to sleep, he reached for his phone and googled *Lotte Wuttcke*. A Wikipedia entry popped up about an archaeologist named Heinrich Wuttcke, who had led excavations across Greece and into parts of Turkey. But Heinrich had died in 1946, over sixty years ago. Still, he wondered if there was some relation. On a whim, he searched for *Heinrich Wuttcke+Lotte Wuttcke*, but that only yielded some old photos of archaeological digs.

Finding himself still awake, he started clicking randomly through YouTube videos. He landed on one clip titled "Squirrels Play a Slot Machine. You Won't Believe What Happens Next!" He clicked on the link. A small red squirrel was lowered into a Perspex box with chutes on both sides. "In a recent study," a male voice began, "scientists tried to discern whether squirrels are intelligent. As you can see, there are two buttons in this box. They both light up once an hour. Pressing the blue button always guarantees a nut. Pressing the red button produces a jackpot of nuts once, but then never again." Dimitri watched as a squirrel hit the red button. An avalanche of nuts came tumbling out of the chute. The squirrel was shown gobbling up its bounty and then maniacally pawing the red button for more. "Once a squirrel has seen the deluge of nuts, it will ignore the blue button from then on. It will keep hitting the red button until it has starved."

Dimitri slept fitfully and woke up feeling tired and hungry. There was coffee in the house, but not much food. He glanced at the wrapped bread Lotte had given him. He pulled back the cloth to discover something more reminiscent of a clod of dirt than a loaf of bread. Its crust was a dark brown, while the inside was almost gray. It didn't look very enticing, but Dimitri was too hungry to care.

"Food is food," he said to himself with a shrug. He spread some butter on it that he had found in the fridge, followed by a glob of acacia honey, and took a bite.

It tasted revolting. The bread was bitter, with a loamy texture and small, light-colored husks that got stuck in his teeth. He tore off a paper towel from the roll on the kitchen counter and spat out the half-chewed mouthful. Then he gulped down some coffee to get rid of the bad taste and swore in Greek. Dimitri picked up the loaf to examine it. It didn't smell bad, and he couldn't see any mold. He pinched out a white chunk and rolled it around between his fingers, trying to discern what it was. Forced to admit defeat, he took the loaf and threw it in the trash.

He considered canceling his meeting with Lotte and turning in early. But when he opened his email, he found another note from her telling him how much she was looking forward to their next rendezvous. He realized he wasn't going to be able to wangle his way out of it so easily. He wrote back, asking if there was a café somewhere closer where they could meet, preferably a little earlier in the evening? He wasn't feeling well, he added, and wasn't up for another late night.

As usual, Lotte took only minutes to reply:

Lieber Dimitri,

Oh, I'm sorry to hear that. I had such a delightful time last night, and was so looking forward to seeing you again. Unfortunately my job does not allow me to meet before 10:00 p.m., but I'd be happy to come to your place if that would work better for you. — LW

He hadn't expected her to be so forward. But he didn't want to offend her, and having to find a new language partner seemed like a hassle. He only had limited time in Berlin. If he failed to become fluent in German, it would be difficult to find work here. That could mean returning to Greece, which seemed to be descending further into chaos by the day. Dimitri wrote back a short note agreeing to her suggestion and giving her his address.

Despite what he had told himself earlier, about half an hour before Lotte was due to arrive, Dimitri caught himself making more of an effort to look nice than the occasion strictly called for. He put on a navy-blue cashmere sweater, fastidiously brushing it to remove any lint or stray hairs. Then he applied some moisturizer to his face, sculpted his hair with wax, and sprayed eau de toilette on the sides of his neck.

Around 10:00 p.m., the doorbell rang. He opened it to reveal Lotte in an elegant shift dress with an Asian pattern, made from a fabric that shimmered between black and dark purple.

"Du siehst gesund aus," he said, which made Lotte chuckle.

"I think you mean: Du siehst umwerfend aus! I look *fabulous*, not *healthy*. But thank you."

Dimitri felt embarrassed to be corrected on a compliment, and sheepishly asked Lotte if she would like a drink.

"I'd love a glass of white," she said as she prowled around the apartment, reaching out to examine various objects. He uncorked a bottle of Chardonnay and poured them each a glass.

Lotte had returned to the kitchen and began surveying the shelves. "I hope you haven't eaten, because I've brought dinner. Another specialty of mine. Is it okay if I start cooking?"

Dimitri was still nauseated at the thought of his aborted breakfast. Without waiting for his response, Lotte started tapping away at the oven display. It seemed to confuse her, and he felt the need to step in. He took a big swig of his wine and walked over to Lotte.

"To be honest," he said, pushing various buttons, "I'm not quite sure how it works either." Nothing about the stove seemed obvious. One button turned on a timer that refused to be set. Another, with a pictogram that resembled a stovetop, switched on the fan.

"Well, at least we know how to cool things down," said Dimitri. Lotte let out an incredulous laugh.

"And they say technology will only make our lives easier," she said, bemused. "Do you have the instructions?"

"I could look them up online."

"Great," she said. "I just need the stove top, a frying pan, and oil. I've already prepared everything else."

Lotte rummaged around in her purse, pulling out a package wrapped in plastic and paper. With a quick motion, she unfolded it to reveal what appeared to be a fish sculpted out of grainy dough.

"Surprise!"

Dimitri stared at it, unable to hide his bewilderment.

"Is something wrong?"

"I'm—just trying to figure out what this is, that's all," he said, navigating around his dismay to spare her feelings.

"It's mock fish!"

He shook his head, still dumbstruck.

"It's my take on mock hare, which is just breaded ground beef mixed with other ingredients to give it body. Americans call it *meatloaf*, the English refer to it as *haslet*. I'm sure there is a Greek version."

"We call it *rolo*," said Dimitri, somewhat reassured.

"Right, so here's my take on it. Instead of making a hare, I've soaked ground feed corn in cod-liver oil to make mock fish! Just wait till you try it. I'll just need a frying pan and spatula if you can find them for me."

As Dimitri searched the kitchen cabinets, Lotte scooped up the wrappings.

"Where is your trash can?"

"It's here," Dimitri said, pulling out a drawer and immediately spotting the discarded loaf. He'd forgotten to get rid of it, and now there was no way to hide it from Lotte. In a split second, she was there dropping the paper into the receptacle.

"I see you didn't like my bread," Lotte said in a matter-of-fact tone.

Dimitri had been caught. He looked up at her, momentarily at a loss for words, but to his surprise, Lotte was smiling.

"Don't worry about it—it's an acquired taste. It's made from acorns. They're very nutritious. They contain six percent fat, roughly the same amount as oats. I'm gathering them right now, in October. They begin to drop as early as September, but it's the same as with apples and plums: the first to fall are mealy. You have to let them lie."

"Is it a Berlin specialty?" he asked.

"You could say that." Lotte laughed. Her voice sounded slightly strained.

"It was—interesting . . . Just a little bit bitter," Dimitri said.

"Yes, it is a bit *pikró*."

"To be honest, I was worried that it might be spoiled. I found these white chunks in the loaf."

"Oh, that's the chalk. It adds a bit of flavor and makes it easier to digest."

"Chalk . . . like in school?" He wasn't sure if Lotte had chosen the right Greek word.

"Right, or like an antacid. That doesn't bother you, does it?"

He pictured her kneading the dough and crumbling a long stick of blackboard chalk into it.

"I suppose not," he said, closing the trash can with the bread still inside.

Luckily, Lotte's mock fish turned out to be a bit better than her bread. They had nearly finished the bottle of wine, and the conversation was less formal than it had been the day before. Dimitri had wanted to ask her more about Berlin, the culture, things he ought to know about, but somehow the conversation drifted back to Lotte's experiences in Greece. "Unemployment was high, economic growth was low," she recalled. "Restaurants had rolled down their shutters and grocery stores had aisle after aisle of empty shelves. People were starving."

Dimitri was curious about what period she was referring to. Greece had a history of economic ups and downs—that had been the case for many years. But thinking back to his youth, Dimitri could not recall starving people. The only stories of famine he had heard were those his grandmother had told him about the time of the occupation, when the Germans had seized all the food supplies. Even fishing had become a punishable offense.

"I wish you could have met my grandmother," Dimitri said. "I think you two would have gotten along."

Lotte bent over and looked at him, intrigued.

"Oh, why is that?"

"She has—and you'll have to forgive my German—the same *peculiarities* as you do. She was very resourceful and liked to make her own things, like recipes and remedies using unusual ingredients."

"Tell me more," Lotte said.

"As a child I was terribly asthmatic, and my grandmother suggested putting an eel in our well as a cure for my illness. And the funny thing," Dimitri said, starting to chuckle, "is that we actually tried it."

Lotte joined in his laughter. "Did it work?"

"Of course not! But not all of her ideas were wacky. My grandmother was a formidable woman. She could create a meal out of nothing and had cures to ease the discomfort of an empty stomach. That's something she taught herself during the war. The Germans, as you may know, purposefully starved everyone because they thought Greeks were *work-shy*, as they put it, and didn't deserve to eat."

Dimitri thought back to his grandmother's stories of seeing people die in the streets, bodies that were scarcely more than skeletons collapsing on the spot. Her recollections were often laced with contempt for the German people. Dimitri wondered what his grandmother would have thought of her grandson moving to Berlin.

What would she have made of Lotte? He looked over at her. There was a strange gleam in Lotte's eyes. Dimitri shifted in his seat. Had he touched a nerve?

"Go on!" she said, somewhat impatiently. "How did your grandmother survive?"

He thought for a moment.

"My grandfather had close ties to the black market, and was able to obtain food and cooking supplies. Olive oil was most valuable—it was like gold. On one occasion my grandmother found herself faced with a real dilemma because of that. A German soldier, a mechanic I think, pounded on their door one night. A car radiator had burst all over his arm and the side of his face, and he demanded to be helped. So my grandfather took him in and tried to use cold water to alleviate the pain. But the soldier begged for something better, so finally my grandfather took out the hidden olive oil and poured some onto the man's burns. Can you imagine? Such a precious substance used to treat the injury of an enemy?"

Lotte looked at him, transfixed.

"Go on!"

Dimitri paused. He wasn't sure he wanted to tell her.

"Well . . . the soldier demanded more oil to take away with him. My grandfather got angry and refused. And the soldier pulled his gun on him and forced him to back down. Then he grabbed their entire supply and took off."

"What happened next?"

"I don't remember. But one of their children didn't survive the war."

He stopped. Lotte had turned away from him. Her shoulder was shaking.

"I have to go," she said, her voice thick with tears.

"I didn't mean to upset you."

"I know you didn't."

Before he could blink, Lotte had jumped up and grabbed her coat.

"Please stay," he said, helplessly.

She looked at him with red eyes.

"I can't," she choked out, before disappearing out the front door. Dimitri heard her heels clicking down the stairs. He went to the window and looked down onto the street. It was drizzling outside; the glow from the streetlights was reflected on the slick asphalt. After a few seconds, Lotte appeared, clutching the collar of her beige trench coat. Dimitri watched as she made her way down the sidewalk. At the corner she suddenly paused and held a hand to an advertising column to steady herself. Then, as Dimitri watched, she slumped to the ground. It happened so slowly that at first he didn't comprehend what was happening right in front of his eyes. He stared, expressionless, at Lotte's motionless body.

Then he suddenly jerked out of his stupor and, without thinking, sprinted out into the stairwell, taking the stairs three at a time. Outside a mist of fine rain sprayed his face. He ran up to the advertising pillar, but when he reached it no one was there. He looked around. The street was empty.

"Lotte!"

There was no reply. He tried to call out again, but he felt his windpipe beginning to constrict. He grabbed his throat, gasping for air. Only when you've had an asthma attack do you realize just how many muscles you have in your torso. His breathing was growing more labored by the minute. No matter how hard Dimitri's muscles worked, it was a struggle to get any oxygen into his lungs. As he sucked desperately at the air, he realized that he had left his emergency inhaler in his suitcase back in the apartment.

Eeh-uh . . . eeh-uh, his bronchial tubes rasped.

He almost dropped the keys as he was trying to open the front door. Once inside, he had to grab onto the bannister to stay on his feet. His apartment was on the fourth floor and he wasn't sure he was going to make it. He gripped the railing tightly and pulled himself up, one step at a time. Brown spots were dancing in front of his eyes. Dimitri was afraid that he was going to pass out, but he somehow made it to the top of the first flight. He looked up at the next set of stairs and, gathering his strength, began ascending them as well. When, after what seemed like ages, he got to the next landing, Dimitri pitched forward headlong to the floor and stayed there, lying flat on his stomach, opening and closing his mouth like a fish thrown onto dry land.

Eeh-uh . . . eeh-uh . . .

As he began to feel himself blacking out, an uncanny calm grew within him like a tiny flicker of light in a pitch-black room. Summoning his last bit of strength, he picked himself back up and continued his climb, dragging himself up the final flight of stairs. On the top floor, he found his door open and his red inhaler lying neatly in a bowl on the entrance table. He spotted it immediately and, taking it into his hands, pushed down the canister and inhaled the cortisone mist. He coughed, feeling the stranglehold around his throat beginning to loosen. Relieved, Dimitri sucked in air. After his breathing had stabilized and his muscles had relaxed, he sat down on his couch, focusing his attention on his inhaler, trying very hard to remember when he had taken it out of his bag.

The half-moon jutted out above the clouds like a crooked menhir. As Dimitri made his way through Prenzlauer Berg, the navigation app on his phone led him down Raumerstrasse, which was crammed with tourists and young people. He elbowed his way through a throng of Asian tourists wearing black hoodies and thick glasses. He couldn't tell if they were students or artists, or composites of both. One of them was rapping in English, his breath fogging in the icy air. Dimitri shivered.

He finally arrived on Helmholtzplatz, and recognized it as being in the same area as the library he had walked into a few days earlier.

Sitting on a bench beneath a streetlight was Lotte. When she looked up to greet him, he could see dark shadows under her eyes. Despite the cold, she was only wearing a raincoat.

"You're shivering," Dimitri said, rubbing his arms with his hands.

"I hadn't expected it to get so cold so quickly," she said.

"Should we go find a warm bar to talk in? I've been so worried about you!"

"I have another place in mind," she said. "Come on, let's go for a walk."

She got up and gave Dimitri a frail smile as she put her arm through his. He was surprised by the gesture, but found it comforting at the same time, and let her lead the way.

"I just don't want to go to a bar today," she said after a moment. "You don't mind, do you?"

"Of course not," Dimitri said. "Whatever you want."

After two or three minutes they had left the brightly lit square behind and drifted together into the darkness. They weaved their way through Prenzlauer Berg, fin-de-siècle apartment blocks rising up on either side of them. An empty tram came clattering past them on Pappelallee on its way to the depot. They reached a wrought-iron gate that opened onto a park. Lotte silently gestured at a rusted copper plaque. Dimitri read the inscription:

Schafft hier das Leben gut und schön, kein Jenseits ist, kein Aufersteh'n

"What exactly does that mean?"

"It translates roughly as: 'Make life here good and beautiful. There is no life beyond the tomb.'"

Dimitri thought about this for a moment. Like almost all Greeks he had been baptized, but he felt bewildered by the pomp and circumstance of the Orthodox church, by the priests with their long beards and the cloying haze of incense. Once he'd breathed in a lungful that had caused an asthma attack so severe the sexton had to call an ambulance. His parents never took him to another Lit-

urgy, nor did Dimitri ever feel the desire to return. He found himself sympathetic to those who lived for this life only.

"I like that there's no mention of God," he said after a moment.

"You're quite right. Why make reference to God if you don't
believe in God's existence?" Lotte replied. "Come, I want to show
you something."

She gave him a gentle tug toward the gravel path. Around them
gray tombstones protruded out of the ground, some bearing names,
others left blank. Now Dimitri recognized where they were: it was
the same park where he had seen the women with their strollers
the other day. Only now it seemed much more like a cemetery.

Lotte stopped in front of a marble slab embedded in the ground.
"This is my husband's grave. He didn't want any kind of religious
symbolism at his funeral."

Dimitri was surprised that they even still performed burials
here. He looked around him. Right across from where they stood
was a playground, and down the path was a coffee stand. The
air was freezing. Suddenly Dimitri felt a tickling in his nose and
sneezed loudly.

"This weather . . ." said Lotte sympathetically, reaching into her
coat. She pulled out a flat metal box and pressed it against his chest.
The object radiated a pleasant heat that spread in broad ripples
through his body.

"Here, this'll warm you up."

"What is this?" he asked as he felt the warmth return.

"It's a nifty little invention: a pocket warmer heated by a burning
charcoal stick."

"But what about you?"

"I'm fine, really. We can pass it back and forth."

Dimitri wondered why there was no smoke coming out of it. He
was about to ask Lotte, but she appeared to be lost in thought.

"I remember," she said after a while, "attending parties where
everyone would have to bring a coal briquette as the entrance fee.

They'd use them to fuel the stove, and then people would dance and sing until everyone was sweating from the heat. It was lovely. Perhaps a little dance now might keep us warm."

Lotte began to sing an old Berlin tune: "Lampenputzer ist mein Vater / Im Berliner Stadttheater / Meine Schwester hat'n Luden / mit drei jroße Seltersbuden."

She gently took Dimitri by the hand and drew him close to her. He gingerly put his arms around her hips. The earth was frosty beneath his feet. When she stopped dancing, they remained in each other's arms. She looked up at him out of the corner of her eye. Dimitri felt an impulse: now or never. He cautiously kissed her on the mouth. For a moment, they remained locked in a tight embrace. Then Lotte gently pushed him away.

"I think I should be honest with you." Lotte paused, looking for words. "What I mean is that I owe you an explanation."

She let go of his hand and looked down at her shoes. "The story you told me yesterday moved me deeply. The havoc the Germans wreaked in Greece during the occupation . . . When you read that at least a hundred thousand people starved, and possibly even more, many more than that—those are numbers I can't even fathom."

"It's a very long time ago now."

"Maybe for you."

There was silence for a moment. Lotte took Dimitri's hand. She quivered, on the brink of tears, but taking a slow breath, she pulled herself together.

"Did you know that during the war, we were gorging ourselves here in Germany on the food that had been requisitioned from occupied countries? But we paid for it. After the war we had to go hungry ourselves. There was almost nothing left—no crops, no infrastructure. 1946 was an especially harsh winter. We had to be resourceful in order to survive. People tore down their wallpaper and boiled it because there were nutrients in the glue. Others ate boiled leather or sawdust. People chopped down trees in the Tiergarten park to fuel their stoves. By then we had been forced to return to Berlin."

"We?" asked Dimitri, suddenly incredulous of her story. Lotte smoothed down her hair. She stared off into the distance.

"Heinrich had been away working in Greece for so long. When we got back, we could we only find a small apartment with no garden where we could have grown vegetables. So I crafted meals out of whatever I could salvage. I was able to survive, but Heinrich just couldn't bring himself to eat some of the things I served up."

Dimitri prickled with sweat. The tenderness that he had felt for her only moments ago had given way to a more apprehensive feeling.

"People don't understand what it means to starve," she continued. "It hurts terribly." She pointed at her stomach and midriff. "Here . . . and here. Your teeth become loose from the vitamin deficiency. Your stomach bloats up. You lose hope in your fellow man, you lose faith in God, you lose everything, until you are nothing but bones and skin."

Dimitri wanted to put his hand on her shoulder and comfort her, but her outburst made him hold back.

As he cautiously turned toward her, he saw something scuttle past them down below. Lotte spun around. Her febrile tension only heightened Dimitri's sense of unease, but he couldn't help but follow her gaze.

"A rat," he muttered under his breath.

"Look, there's another!"

Dimitri spotted the second rat, scurrying from the opposite direction. Both rats seemed to be drawn to something hidden between the tombstones. Lotte chased after them, leaving Dimitri standing alone. He swore to himself and at all the atheists buried beneath his feet, then followed Lotte. When he reached her, he saw that she was holding something cupped in her hands—a rat frozen in rigor mortis. Its head and claws were twisted at crooked angles, its lips curled back to expose two needle-sharp teeth and a sliver of purple gum. Only its tail was slack, dangling between Lotte's fingers like a fat grub.

"Lotte," Dimitri said softly. "What's going on?"

Lotte held the rat out toward him as if it were a dead child. She gave Dimitri a challenging look.

"My love, where do you draw the line? At bread made from acorns? Fish from cattle feed? Horse meat? Dog meat?"

Somewhere in the distance, a fire truck howled past. Lotte was briefly still, fixating on the rat with a feverish glint in her eye.

"Aftó pou epiválame se állous laoús, tha éprepe na eímaste se thési na to antéxoume kai oi ídioi!" she called out to Dimitri in flawless Greek. *What we inflicted on other peoples, we should have been able to bear ourselves!*

With a squelching sound, Lotte bit into the rat's hairless torso. A colorless liquid ran out of the corner of her mouth. Then she vomited.

BALL LIGHTNING

THE BIG DECISIONS IN LIFE are binary—one or zero, plus or minus, kids or no kids, surgery or no surgery, to help or not to help. And often we don't realize that we're at a crossroads; only in retrospect does the moment become resonant with significance.

On a balmy day in April, two Ph.D. students were sitting in a garden in Steglitz preparing for a graduate course. Anne Berckenbrink and Alex Engel knew neither that one day they would be married nor that they were going to kiss in exactly three minutes' time. If anyone had told them, they would have been utterly astonished.

"My grandma saw ball lightning once," Alex said, looking pensively at a tuft of cloud drifting past in the sky.

"Does that even exist?" Anne asked skeptically.

"My grandmother was a chemist. She was very rational. I'm sure she didn't imagine it."

"What did it look like?"

"A crackling sphere, about the size of a handball. It came in through the open window."

"That's pretty scary."

"The thing shot all around the room. My grandmother pressed herself up against the wall because she knew intuitively that it was dangerous."

"And then what happened?"

"I don't know. Probably the lightning just fizzled out."

Alex wanted to tell her more about his grandmother, but a mild spring drizzle began to fall. Then the two young people were taken by surprise as billions of fat drops came pelting down out of the sky. Giggling and shrieking, they hurriedly gathered up their papers and fled to the living room. With flushed cheeks, they gazed back out through the open terrace door at the beech trees whose leaves were now buckling under the barrage of raindrops. Around them the world was filled with new sounds—the distant bark of the dog next door, the gurgling of the water in the gutters, a car tire plowing through a fresh puddle.

Anne noticed that Alex was standing a little closer to her than usual. They breathed in and out, their faces close together, at the mercy of the weather and their hormones.

Anne's long eyelashes, almost imperceptibly, fluttered.

She was waiting for a decision: yes or no.

Cautiously Alex drew her to him and kissed her. She let it happen.

Only after a small eternity did they break apart.

When the rain stopped, they stood motionless in the doorway, not speaking. A garbage truck came rumbling past outside. Beyond the invisible circle that enclosed Anne and Alex—the two of them in its center, gazing into each other's widened pupils—everyday life in the Berlin suburbs continued as usual.

The first decision made, the couple now made a second—moving from the living room into Anne's bedroom. As neither of them had anticipated this course of events, a succession of mishaps ensued: there were blinds that wouldn't close, a bra that wouldn't open, and the excitement had turned Anne's hands ice-cold, which she felt terribly embarrassed about. She needn't have worried, however, since Alex was completely preoccupied with the rest of her body.

In the midst of this intimate moment the door to Anne's bedroom was flung open. The brass door handle hit the wall so hard that an oval piece of plaster fell clean off. Anne and Alex were jolted out of their trance; instantly they were transformed back into the self-conscious, cerebral people that they had been just moments before.

Anne's mother, Maria Berckenbrink, was standing in the doorway.

"This place is haunted!" she shouted, her voice quavering.

Alex seemed paralyzed by the sudden shock; Anne felt him shrivel up inside her. She could have sunk through the floor in shame. What was her mother even thinking—how dare she? Anne wanted to yell something unspeakable at her, which would have been completely out of character, but Maria had already disappeared again.

"I'm so sorry," Anne whispered to her brand-new boyfriend, who was rummaging through the sheets in search of his boxer shorts.

"I should go," he mumbled.

"No, no, please stay."

Even before Anne had had the chance to change his mind, footsteps could be heard outside the door. Just like in the circus, where the clown whose antics weren't even funny the first time around pokes his head through the curtains for an encore, Maria stumbled back into the bedroom and turned on the light. In the glare of the four halogen spots, the couple's nakedness was illuminated down to the last detail. In a reflex, Alex pulled the sheet over his hips, while Anne got up and covered her modesty with a bathrobe.

"What the fuck," Alex mumbled.

"What's taking so long?" Maria slurred at her daughter.

Anne could smell the alcohol on her mother's breath all the way from the bed.

"Mama, have you lost your mind?"

"This is not a drill, this is the real thing!" Maria shouted, her voice cracking.

Her heavily powdered face seemed grotesquely contorted, like a Japanese Kabuki mask. She was a small, portly woman with dyed-blonde curls and raggedy fingernails painted red. A long time ago, people had found her to be a pleasant, sweet woman, but fate had dealt her a bad hand, and little by little the pleasant aspects of her character had receded and less likeable ones had risen to the surface.

Anne was already familiar with her mother's moods when she was in this drunken state, and so she knew that kicking up a fuss would only make things much worse. Desperate to avoid that kind of escalation in front of her new boyfriend, she acquiesced to her fate, seething with anger.

"Okay, five minutes—not a *second* longer."

Maria nodded; her smug satisfaction at the fact that her daughter was humoring her request was clearly visible. Anne turned back to face Alex, held up the five fingers of her right hand, and breathed a barely audible "wait!"

Barefoot, she followed her mother up to the second floor.

In contrast to Anne's clean and tidy realm, utter chaos ruled here: books were stacked up in front of an overflowing bookshelf, a pile of dirty laundry beside them; in the kitchen, dirty dishes spilled out of the sink.

"Over there!" Maria said, pointing an accusing finger at the wall above her trashed desk. Two prints of photos she had taken on a cruise to the North Cape were hanging there. One showed a glacier slowly disgorging into a lake; the other showed the city of Bergen in the dawn light.

"What?" Anne asked, annoyed.

"Don't you see? The pictures have been switched around."

"Mama, cut it out, they've always been that way."

"No, the one with the houses was on the left. Look closer."

Anne's eyes followed Maria's outstretched index finger. Above the city panorama, which had been taken in landscape format, it was indeed possible to make out a pale spot on the wall which, with some imagination, could be from the portrait-format picture of the glacier.

"Maybe you switched them around yourself?" Anne offered spitefully.

Her mother's eyes blazed with anger.

"Why would I have done that? That's bullshit!" she said.

Anne shrugged her shoulders.

"Mama, I can't help you."

She turned abruptly on her heels and left Maria standing in the study, so plastered that she was having a hard time maintaining her balance and had to hold onto the back of a chair for support.

Alex came towards her in the hallway. He was fully dressed and had thrown his coat around his shoulders.

"Alex . . ."

"Next time, let's meet at my place, okay?" he said gently.

✖

The suited man leaned back in his armchair. A slight breeze blew through the tilted-open window and stirred the lace curtains. He turned his attention to Alex, who was sitting on the opposite side of the table.

"Herr Engel, allow me to ask you a question first."

"Sure, go ahead, Herr Lorentz."

"There's a psychology exercise—I'm sure you've heard of it—in which the patient is given words that he has to spontaneously associate with other words—like *duck/beak*, or *house/roof*."

"Yes, I've heard of that."

"I'd like to play a round of this association game with you. The word that I've picked out for you is: *Stasi*."

Alex kept an expressionless face.

"Well? What was it that came to mind?"

The two men—one old, one young—looked at each other wordlessly.

"Well, East Germany's Ministry for State Security, of course."

"Yes, that's what the Stasi is objectively. But what does *Stasi* bring to your mind *subjectively*? Big Brother? Betrayal? Snitches? You surely associate the Stasi with ugly images."

"I look at it from an academic point of view, as a historian," Alex replied neutrally.

"But you must have a personal opinion."

"I'm writing a Ph.D. history thesis, not a bill of indictment. I've asked for this meeting because I'd like to learn firsthand what it was like to work for the Stasi."

"Whatever you say. Alright, then, pay attention. I'll tell you everything, but I won't repeat myself."

Alex looked at Lorentz expectantly.

"Please continue."

"I signed up with the Stasi because of my father. He was in the GDR's secret police himself. He'd been a Nazi, you know. Not by choice—he was first and foremost a socialist. But he was a surveying technician, one with a good reputation, so the Nazis, the Gestapo, took him to their headquarters. He was given a choice: join the party or lose his job. They wouldn't release him until he made his choice either. Can you imagine how afraid my mother must have been?"

Alex shook his head lightly.

"The moment my father was a free man again, he began systematically to plan their escape. That's how my parents ended up arriving in Moscow in 1935."

"Why did your family come back?"

"That's a fair question—after all, I suppose we could just have stayed in the Soviet Union, where my father was welcome to stay and had a job. But the war had left Germany a destroyed and morally bankrupt state. In the Western occupation zones the Nazis were able to seamlessly resume their pre-party careers. On the other side of the Iron Curtain, however, people were working toward a more just and honest system. Of course, this is the opposite of how history now remembers the GDR—as a place whose citizens were oppressed and penned in behind the Wall."

Lorentz was now looking closely at Alex to see if he agreed.

"Go on," Alex replied calmly.

"Anyway, my family returned to Berlin in 1946, and my father signed up with a construction brigade—basically a clean-up crew for the pile of rubble that Berlin had become—volunteering to do back-breaking work for a pittance. The job did allow him into every conceivable corner of the Russian sector, where he'd hear what people thought about socialism and the occupation. My father passed some of these things on. He wasn't interested in spying on his countrymen, but did want to protect the young, fragile republic from a resurgence of Nazism. Eventually, the Ministry for State Security recruited him because they needed proven antifascists like him.

"As one of the very first students to attend the universities of the new nation I, too, wanted to help the GDR to flourish. I graduated with a degree in biology, but my real talent lay elsewhere—I had inherited my father's knack for obtaining information. It was an ability that he encouraged me to put to use working for the Ministry for State Security. I wasn't *recruited* to the Stasi so much as following in my father's footsteps, for the same reasons he had joined himself: a sense of pride and a need to protect this fledgling new state."

✖

After the embarrassing disaster in Anne's mother's house, the two lovers decided to meet again on neutral territory. Alex chose the most innocuous place he could think of: the Mango Tango ice-cream parlor on Lilienthalstrasse. The walls of the newly opened store were clad in pastel-green tiles that came shoulder high. In the background, a guy who looked vaguely like Mark Zuckerberg was fiddling with a chrome espresso machine, foaming up one latte after the other for a clientele that seemed to consist largely of pregnant education majors.

Alex ordered one scoop of chocolate in a cup out of habit. Anne was feeling more adventurous and opted for one scoop of pistachio and one scoop of plantain.

"Is that good?" Alex asked suspiciously.

"So-so."

They went over to a high table in the corner.

"So, um," Alex began carefully, resting his hand lightly on Anne's arm—a feather-light touch. "Why are you living with your mother?"

The question embarrassed her.

"It's hard, having to live at home again at twenty-eight. I want to finish my thesis without having to juggle a part-time job to make rent. It's just temporary."

"You don't need to justify it, I was just curious."

"And it kind of lets me keep an eye on her. She's drinking more than ever. I'm afraid that . . ."

Anne faltered. She felt forlorn, suddenly overwhelmed by the problems that she was carrying around with her. Alex drew her to him. His girlfriend leaned into the warmth of the embrace.

"It's okay," he whispered gently.

After they'd been standing like that for a while, and their ice cream had melted in their cups, Anne's mood lifted.

"My mom's had a shitty life."

"Because your stepfather walked out on her, you mean?"

"No, not just because of that. It started much earlier, when she was still back East. She was a dissident, and they made her life a living hell. When none of that had any effect, finally they stripped her of her citizenship. She didn't want to leave at all—she had to leave all her friends behind, and then she was stuck by herself out here with a small child . . ."

"That sounds pretty rough."

Anne put on a brave smile.

"She's always been a rebel, my mom."

"Good for her—only very few people had that kind of courage."

"But now . . ." Anne swallowed. "She's letting herself go too much."

The next morning around eleven, Anne unlocked the door of the small rowhouse and went inside. She had spent the night at Alex's—a wonderful night. Now, the sharp scent of high-proof alcohol greeted her the second she stepped into the hallway. In these moments she felt a white-hot anger rise up in her. Why couldn't her mother be like other mothers?

She tiptoed into the living room. Maria was lying on the sofa in a dressing gown, out cold. Her lipstick was smudged, her hair a tangled mess. It was hard to tell how long she'd been lying there like that—all night, at least. Maria herself wouldn't be able to say, because she tended to black out after her binges. Anne bent over to check that she was breathing. Her mother smelled like cheap whiskey. Anne was repulsed by the whole picture. She despised this person, this wreck of a human being.

She decided right there and then to do a raid—a thorough one. She knew full well that Maria hid her bottles. She also knew where the largest depository was, because she had recently watched her mother open the grandfather clock and put something inside it. Sure enough, she found six whiskey flasks stacked up in there. She emptied the contents into the toilet and threw the bottles in the glass recycling container, where they shattered with a loud crash.

She knew there had to be other hiding places—there was nothing in the world that her mother feared more than the moment when her stash ran out. There was sure to be an emergency supply in her bedroom.

The first place Anne looked was under the bed, but that was too obvious. The wardrobe was in a state of utter chaos, but there was nothing in there either. She almost overlooked the orange plastic bottle on the bedside table. There was no reason for her mother to keep shampoo here, and so Anne had a sudden flash of inspiration. She unscrewed the top and sniffed the mouth of the bottle— this wasn't hair-care product, it was Stroh rum, at least 100 proof. She walked over to the washbasin and poured the brown liquid down the sink. So what if her mother had to suffer, go through withdrawal? She had to suffer too, every day, every moment, every blink of an eye she spent in this house.

"What the hell do you think you're doing?"

Anne shrank. Maria was standing right behind her, a mug in her right hand. She fixed her daughter with the glittering, wrathful gaze of a vengeance goddess from antiquity.

If there was anything that drove Anne—normally the epitome of gentleness—berserk, it was Maria's penchant for theatricality. She snatched the mug out of her mother's hand.

"What are you drinking?" she snapped.

"Coffee."

"There's maybe a teaspoon of coffee in there, the rest is whiskey."

"Let me have my Irish coffee!" Maria said indignantly. She made a grab for her mug, which resulted in a minor tussle. Amid the push and pull, most of the contents spilled onto the carpet. When Anne refused to let go, her mother finally gave up.

"This is still my house, you know!" she yelled, her voice tipping into an affected falsetto.

"Mama, you'll end up killing yourself with this shit!"

"Get out!"

Maria pointed at the door, her eyes afire.

"Leave!"

Anne left her mother standing in the bedroom and slammed the door shut behind her.

✖

"Are we recording?"

"Just a moment, Herr Lorentz."

"Seems like it was a whole lot easier back when we still used tapes . . ."

Alex placed the digital recorder between them.

"There! All set."

With a nod, Alex indicated that Lorentz should proceed.

"Before we get started, there's something I'd like to say."

"Go ahead."

Lorentz cleared his throat and watched the corresponding spike in the sound wave on the recorder's display.

"I don't assume that people are by nature bad. When I say that I—like my father—worked for the GDR's secret police because I wanted to protect our country from internal and external enemies, that doesn't mean that I saw every upstanding citizen as a potential saboteur. You saw different things at different levels. Most people who enter the Stasi begin as an *informal collaborator* or IM. In this capacity, I considered it my primary responsibility to see to it that people who had wrongly ended up in the crosshairs of the authorities were exonerated."

"Can you give me an example?"

"Well, one time my handler at the ministry asked me to keep an eye on a fellow student who was suspected of disseminating prohibited literature. I knew this young man and liked him, and I was soon able to disprove the suspicions against him. The proceedings were dropped."

"And how often did things like that happen?" asked Alex.

"Often enough that my conscience is clear. I'm even friendly today with a number of people I helped keep out of trouble. It wasn't until my trial period as a rookie *Blauer* or 'blue carder' had ended, and I switched to a permanent position with the ministry, that I began to encounter people who were undeniably engaged in subversive activities. But just because the Stasi went after such people didn't make us monsters. In every society, there are citizens who staunchly refuse to comply with the rules. The West focused on punishment, throwing people in jail after they broke the law. In the East, we were more interested in prevention, apprehending people who were likely to commit crime. We had our finger on the pulse of the population— we knew who to keep an eye on. It may not have been fair in the conventional sense, I freely admit that, but I don't feel guilty about it."

"At what point would you stop monitoring and take action?"

"If an IM reported a new member of a seditious group, we would summon the person to the local station 'to clarify an issue.' We'd make insinuations in the conversation, no more, without ever becoming explicit. In most cases that was enough to intimidate them into terminating their activities."

"And what if it wasn't?"

"In those cases, we would conduct house searches where we'd seize incriminating material. Not while the person was home, mind you. We operated very sensitively, always making sure to cover our tracks. Sometimes we would install surveillance equipment—bugs—so that we'd know in good time if there was danger on the horizon.

"Even when there was an overwhelming amount of evidence, there were still ways to avoid bringing in the judiciary. Rather than banging a gavel, we preferred to employ a rapier. If small interventions didn't work, we cranked the dial, so to speak. The tame ones we frightened; the wild ones we broke."

"When you wanted to take more . . . severe action, what did that mean in concrete terms?"

"You mean when we *had to* take more severe action. Usually we would try to isolate the person with targeted measures—not just in a physical sense, but also mentally, emotionally. You could totally incapacitate someone, erode their sense of self-worth. There was no fail-safe recipe for how you did that; we had to be creative. I came to see myself as something of an artist."

"How do you mean?"

"There was one target subject who was deeply neurotic and paranoid. While she was away at work, we let ourselves into her apartment and moved things around: a chair to a different room, a different book on the bedside table, clean clothes in the laundry basket, and so on. The person in question ended up doubting her own sanity and finally had herself committed. We had neutralized her without ever becoming visible. I'm still proud of how elegantly we solved that case."

✖

Anne didn't see her mother again until two days later. She'd been staying with Alex in the meantime, who lived in a small two-bedroom apartment in Tempelhof. There was nothing she wanted less than to go back to the house in Steglitz, but that was where her books were, along with her clothes and some other things that she couldn't do without in her day-to-day life.

She wanted to avoid running into her mother at all costs. Ideally she would like to disappear from her life altogether. Anne felt certain at this point that she wouldn't be able to solve Maria's problems. She couldn't manage to pull her mother out of the morass; if anything, her mother was dragging her down with her. The situation was unsustainable.

Anne carefully unlocked the door and crept into the hallway like a burglar. There had been a change in the weather over the weekend and it was making everything seem even gloomier than it already was. In the living room the old grandfather clock struck two-thirty. Anne went down to her room and began packing underwear, paperwork, and makeup into a backpack. She went about it calmly and systematically. As she was pulling open the dresser to take out pants, socks, and her crimson cashmere pullover, there was a knock on the door. Anne flinched inwardly.

Clearly her mother had excellent ears.

When Anne opened the door, Maria was standing in front of her, her face streaked with tears. She looked pale, her cheeks sunken. Nothing was left of the imperious manner that made her so unbearable when she was drunk.

"I'm sorry, I'm so, so sorry," she sobbed, by now completely hysterical.

The disdain that Anne had been feeling for her mother dissolved into thin air. Instead she was suddenly overcome by a terrible pity for her. Her heart contracted.

"Mama, I had to do it," Anne said guiltily.

Maria threw her arms around her daughter's neck, hanging there like a wet sack. Her shoulders were shaking. She smelled of stale sweat. Anne held her for a moment, and then carefully disentangled herself.

"You have to stop drinking this much. It's killing you."

"I promise."

"At least try."

Maria pulled a crumpled handkerchief from her sleeve and began to elaborately wipe her nose. While she was doing this, her gaze suddenly fell upon an object that attracted her attention. She put the handkerchief down and smiled sadly, a large teardrop running down from her left eye and clinging to the tip of her nose.

"Look, I didn't imagine it after all," she choked out.

"What, mama?" asked Anne, perplexed.

"That there are ghosts here."

Maria pointed at the framed butterflies that she'd brought back for her daughter from her first big trip. The iridescent creatures were pinned to black velvet.

"What do you mean? That's just that old thing from Peru."

"Pumpkin, look, they're the wrong way around."

Anne took a closer look at the rectangular glass box. Her mother was right—the little legs of the insects were pointing upward; their heads and antennae down. But so what?

Her mother had already lost so many brain cells to alcohol. Did Anne really have to indulge her every absurd whim?

"Someone probably just took them down to look at them and then hung them back wrong," Anne said coldly.

"You mean that new boyfriend of yours? I don't trust him anyway, with that research he's up to—why is he doing that? Why dig around in the dirt?"

"Leave Alex out of it."

"If it wasn't him, it was the ghosts." Maria wiped the tears from her face.

"Mama, there are bigger things to worry about."

✖

"Does your mother really believe in ghosts?" Alex asked, putting a spoonful of ice cream into his mouth.

"When she's drunk she gets all kinds of crazy-ass ideas. But this one isn't completely new. She told me once that her apartment in East Berlin was haunted—things disappeared and turned up again in the wrong places."

"That reminds me of something I heard recently."

"What's that?"

"Just that not all ghosts are imagined. Sometimes there are tangible phenomena."

"Like your grandmother and her ball of lightning, you mean."

"Something like that. But lightning that also strikes."

"You're being cryptic."

"I know. I'm sorry. Just forget I said anything."

✖

Mother and daughter are sitting on the sofa. The mother looks bleary-eyed, her face blotchy from crying.

"Why are you drinking so much?" the daughter wants to know.

"Because the ghosts are back."

"There are no ghosts."

"Then call it the past."

"The past is over."

"No. It's just like it was back then."

"What happened back then?"

"First the ghosts came, and then they threatened to take you away from me."

The mother sobs.

"You were so small and helpless. How could they even say something like that?"

"Such pigs."

"They said either I packed my things and disappeared or they'd put you in a home."

"Wow."

"I gave up my passport the next day."

The daughter takes the mother's hand.

They breathe deeply, in and out.

"Mama, it's all such a long time ago."

The daughter gives the mother a pleading look.

"Yes, but I still feel so lost sometimes. Please, please stay with me!"

"Alex doesn't want to take me away from you."

"I know."

"He's not the Stasi."

"I don't want to lose you."

"I don't want to lose you either."

Mother and daughter hold on to each other and cry. After some time, the mother, exhausted, puts her legs up and falls asleep with the daughter gently stroking her hair.

NEEDLE AND THREAD

"THERE ARE WOLVES AND THERE are wiener dogs!" bellowed Christophe, founder and CEO of Nectar, as he stalked past his VPs lined up in front of him. It was late—many of the other employees had long gone home—but this was a war-room meeting. After months of speculation, Nectar, a rising e-commerce start-up, was about to launch its IPO. Reports that Nectar's logistics department wasn't able to cope with the company's rapid growth had Christophe on high alert. He paced in front of his top aides, his hands clasped behind his back.

"Right from day one we have to go in tanks rolling, boots on the ground. If the competition hires two hundred extra people and grows their team to four hundred in a month, you need to hire six hundred, and then twelve hundred. Hit hard! Poach their customers, roll out image campaigns, put your own logistics in place. Don't count on me to be your daddy and have a plan for you. You guys need to be the ones with the plan, and it has to be one that leads to total victory. I'll give you as much money as you want—I'll get a whole shipping container full of it and empty it out over your heads. Don't be pussies, be heroes, and fight like heroes—to the death."

Christophe stopped pacing and turned to his VP of logistics, who was standing at his side. He flicked his wrist to check the time.

"Armin, it's almost 8:00 p.m. You must be hungry. What are you in the mood for?"

Armin thought for a moment and swallowed audibly. "Sushi?"

Christophe's face smiled, but his eyes were cold. "Sushi?! Do wolves eat fucking sushi?"

"No."

"I'm going to ask you again. What are you in the mood for?"

"Wiener dogs."

"Louder! What are you fucking craving?"

"Wiener dogs!"

Christophe pulled Armin into a tight hug. "I always knew you were a wolf," he said in a tender whisper. Then he let him go and surveyed the group, his eyes gleaming. "That's why I hired all of you!" Christophe roared. "You're all wolves! If anyone can pull off this IPO launch, it's you guys. Success means our wildest dreams coming true. Money, power, influence. I don't need to tell you what it means if we fail, because I know you aren't going to let that happen."

Christophe could make his VPs break into a sweat, but to the rest of the company they were untouchable. In Nectar's language, they were known as the *Praetorians*, a personal guard to the company's mercurial CEO. They all had immaculate résumés: degrees from prestigious universities, positions at global conglomerates and consultancy firms. They could have signed with any company in the world and earned six figures right from the start. Instead, Christophe had wooed them with major stock portfolios and swanky benefits, and lured them into signing with Nectar—his company, his baby—on the promise that it would be the next Amazon.

To distinguish itself in the crowded online marketplace, Nectar sold both commercial and artisanal products—Amazon and Etsy all in one, at twice the speed. Someone in New York could order items as disparate as a flat-screen TV shipped from Seoul and shoes made by Indonesian cobblers and expect them both within forty-eight hours. But if the company was going to remain successful, it needed to be even speedier. The slightest hint of bad press could result in an IPO that opened with plummeting stock. Christophe made clear that this issue needed to be addressed immediately. "Be prepared to earn a whole lot of frequent-flyer miles."

The leader of the Praetorians was Björn, the VP of global operations and Christophe's right-hand man. He'd been one of Nectar's first hires, and saw the company as his chance at making the kind of fortune others had made when companies such as Facebook and PayPal had launched their IPOs. On late nights like these, he tended to avoid looking at his phone, doing his best to duck the volley of texts from his wife, which became increasingly hostile the longer he was away.

Björn was heading for the door when Christophe called him back into the meeting room. He found his boss looking down at an iPad lying on the conference table. Christophe beckoned for Björn to join him. A map of Chile filled the screen.

"Why is it so difficult to make shopping so easy?" he asked.

"What do you mean?"

"I mean this country at the ass-end of the world that is supposed to be our hub for South America. Our poor distribution is *killing* us in that market. Our ships go into Valparaíso, but that's way too far south."

He pointed at the port city, more than a thousand miles away from Chile's border with Peru.

"It's ridiculous. It's fine for fulfilling same-day orders in Santiago, we can even fulfill most orders from Argentina in twenty-four hours, but orders from Ecuador, Bolivia, Peru, take us a whole other day."

"I know. But Armin's on top of it, isn't he?"

"Well, apparently the Chilean contractors have suggested some new warehouse to him. But I've got a gut feeling there'll be something wrong with it."

"Why?"

Christophe pointed to an area inland from the coastal city of Antofagasta.

"It's somewhere around here, apparently. They said it's already built and ready to go, but it's in the middle of the desert. I think Armin's being taken for a ride. Do you know Spanish?"

"A few words. Hola. Gracias. Corona."

"Great. You'll need them in Chile."

"You mean you want me to go check it out?"

Christophe looked up from the map and placed a heavy hand on Björn's shoulder.

"I need someone on the ground who I can trust. And the only person I trust is you."

As he stepped out of the glass reception area onto Hackescher Markt, an icy wind buffeted Björn's face. He turned up his collar and strode to his car. He'd been running late that morning and had left his black Alfa Romeo in a no-parking zone; now there was a parking ticket tucked under the windshield wipers. He cursed out loud.

As he fought his way through the Saturday night rush hour toward Schöneberg, he dialed his wife's number.

"What's taking so long?" Tanja's voice came through the speaker phone. She sounded exhausted.

"I'll be with you in ten minutes. Is Alena asleep?"

"No, she's scared," she said, annoyed.

"Scared of what?"

Tanja sighed. "She can tell you herself when you get in."

She hung up without saying goodbye.

Moments later, Björn was steering toward the wrought-iron gates that led down to the underground parking garage. They had moved here several months before. Björn had purchased a loft space early after being tipped off that an investor was planning to convert a former mental hospital into luxury apartments. The main building had retained its turn-of-the-century facade, while the complex had been filled with spacious, modern apartments and the subterranean garage. The other residents in the neighborhood scoffed at the imposing frontages, and someone had clumsily sprayed "Stop the gentrification of Schöneberg!" onto a wall. Björn considered this nothing more than thinly veiled jealousy.

Björn had wanted a home fit for Alena to grow up in, maybe even with a brother or sister at some point. When he heard about the refurbishment, he'd been first in line to claim one of the apartments. They presented him with the blueprint and invited him to take his pick. It was clear that one was the standout—a first-floor space that jutted out from the building.

Björn parked his car and took the elevator up to the first floor. The sound of his footsteps on the marble floor rose up into the atrium behind the stairs. His apartment was at the end of the hallway. He opened it, took off his coat and threw it over a chair in the entryway. The overhead lights were dimmed; local radio was on in the background. Tanja was sitting on the violet designer sofa. Her legs were drawn up, and she was cradling a bulbous wine glass in her right hand, half-filled with iced Pouilly-Fumé. With her other hand, she slid the bishop on the chess app on her tablet several squares forward, advancing it to threaten the queen. Tanja always had it set to the highest level of difficulty, which gave the CPU up to five minutes to think. Today she'd been forced on the defensive several times because she kept getting distracted and it took a while to get back into it each time.

Tanja had a pretty face and the broad shoulders of a trained swimmer. She had been born and raised in Moscow, but had relocated to Germany in 1997 to study mathematics at the Free University of Berlin. By the time Björn met her, Tanja had her Ph.D. and had become Nectar's first programmer. She'd been working there for several years already when he joined the company; she had even been the one to show him around. He was taken by her straightforward and direct manner. Their relationship followed a very straight path, from moving in, to marriage, and finally pregnancy. An unwavering pragmatic, Tanja had suggested she stay at home to raise Alena for the first few years, while Björn would be the bread-winner. But this division of labor was clearly getting to her more with every passing day. She was the kind of person whose moods and feelings were obvious just from looking at her. Right now she was looking glum.

"You're late—even by your standards," she said without looking up from her iPad.

"I'm sorry. You know how hard it is to get a meeting with Christophe," Björn said, replying to the unspoken accusation.

The computer moved its knight, blocking the diagonal that Tanja had just opened up.

"Do you want to go and pay some attention to your daughter now?"

Björn knew that was not a question.

"Of course, I'm on it," he said in the same decisive voice he usually reserved for conference calls.

The door of his five-year-old daughter's bedroom had been left slightly ajar to allow a little light to spill in from the hallway. Björn pushed it open soundlessly. He found Alena buried under her duvet up in her loft bed.

"Baby girl?"

"Daddy?"

"Are you still awake? It's late. You know you have ballet in the morning."

"I'm scared," she said in a reedy little voice.

"What are you scared of, my love?"

"I'm scared of the *lady*," Alena said, gesturing toward the chair across from the bed.

"What lady?"

"The lady who lives here."

"There's no lady who lives here, darling."

"There *is*, daddy. Why is she sitting there? Why won't she go away?"

Björn jumped up and turned the light on. "I don't see anyone here."

Alena blinked. In the bright glare of the ceiling light, her pupils narrowed to pinpricks. Her sandy hair stood up wildly around her head. She looked like a crazy professor.

"Okay, where is this lady?"

Alena peered out over the edge of the bed and surveyed the empty chair.

"What's the lady sewing?" she asked, furrowing her brow.

"There's no one there. Listen, I'm here now, sweetie. I'll hold your hand until you're asleep and when I leave I'll take the chair with me, okay?"

"Okay."

A little hand crept out from underneath the duvet. He took it and gave it a gentle squeeze. Alena's fear seemed to be ebbing away.

"Daddy, when will I get a loose tooth?"

"Time to get some sleep."

Alena rolled over obediently. Björn held her hand until he heard her breathing begin to slow. His own heart rate, however, was increasing. He knew that Tanja wasn't going to be happy to hear that he now had to go to Chile.

As he sat there, perfectly still, this worry was joined by another, more complex feeling. Alena's room suddenly felt claustrophobic, a cube with no opening, walled off from the rest of the world—like one of those strange spatial anomalies that have no exterior, just an interior, and which can be calculated on paper but cannot be depicted graphically.

Since his daughter was now sleeping soundly, he got up, carefully lifted up the chair, and tiptoed back to the living room with it. As he was putting it down in a corner, he felt something snag on the sleeve of his blazer. He looked down and noticed a single long gray hair dangling from one of his cuff buttons.

"Did someone stop by?" he asked.

"A male someone? I wish," Tanja replied drily, her chessboard now sparsely occupied.

"Weird," Björn said, holding up the hair to examine it. He went into the kitchen to throw it out. When he returned, Tanja was sitting on the couch, sipping her wine, the iPad face down.

"You win?"

"I lost."

"Listen," Björn began abruptly, screwing up his courage. "Christophe has asked me to go on a business trip. I'll be leaving in a few days."

Tanja rounded on him. "Where? How long?" she snapped.

"Chile. A few days. A week at most."

"Chile?! What the hell is in Chile?"

"I need to go look at a warehouse." He felt lame saying it. "But I—"

"Now you listen!" Tanja said, cutting him off. "You have responsibilities to this family too. I've put my career on hold, fine, but that doesn't mean that bringing up Alena should just be down to me."

"Tanja, please . . ."

"I need a job. But day-care gets out at 2:00 p.m. How am I supposed to work around that?"

"Work from home?"

Tanja shook her head. "No! I need to get out of this house. There's something oppressive about it."

Björn looked around, bewildered, but he didn't say anything.

"Listen—it can't go on like this," she said vehemently.

Tanja came from a culture in which, as a matter of course, women would go back to work once their child was a few months old. And she was an excellent coder, a profession that she loved.

"I'm climbing the walls just sitting around here. I'm going to start applying for jobs tomorrow," she said with sudden force.

"Is the day-care center going to let us enroll Alena full-time?"

"Only when I can prove that I have a full-time job. Until then we'll have to hire a nanny to take some of the weight off me. And soon, like tomorrow."

"Alright, let's do that then," Björn said meekly.

The morning before Björn was due to leave for Chile, Armin emailed to report that they hadn't gotten as far with the new site as they had hoped. *Maybe we shouldn't go until later. At the moment, the distribution center is little more than a crumbling ruin. But don't worry, I'm on it.* Björn's heart sank. Somehow he'd missed what Christophe had noticed right away.

It took Björn fifteen minutes and a dozen calls to finally reach Armin, who answered with a faux-jovial hello.

Björn fired a loud "bullshit!" at him, followed by a slew of orders.

"We are going to fucking go over there, and we are not coming back until we have a distribution center in place. And yes, this *is* your responsibility, and you are coming with me!" He hung up and threw his phone on his chair with such force that it bounced right onto the floor.

Björn reached down to see if he had damaged his device. There was a large crack running slantwise across the screen. "Shit!" he muttered under his breath.

As if prompted by Björn's swearing, the phone started to buzz and vibrate frenetically. Even through the cracked screen, he could make out Christophe's name on the caller ID.

"Christophe!" he said, nervously. "I just got an email from Armin."

"About?"

"He needs more time to fix Chile."

"Don't play me for a goddamn idiot, bro. We don't *have* time. What's being done to take care of the situation?"

"I'm taking care of it. I'm taking Armin with me. We'll be on a plane tomorrow."

"You'll be on a plane tonight." Christophe hung up. For a moment, Björn held his breath, stunned. The *ding* of an incoming text sounded from his phone. It was from Tanja. *I found us a nanny. I want you to meet her. What time will you be home?*

Björn sat back in his chair and let out a deep breath. For a moment he just watched time passing from his desk, his mind going blank. In front of him the employees scuttled around like ants in an ant-hill, some rushing to meetings, others clustering around the water cooler. None of them had the slightest clue that their employment depended on a lousy distribution center. It was absurd, and so was the idea of being on a plane in a few hours' time. He called his assistant and had her change his flight, then texted Tanja back to say that he would be home in the next twenty minutes.

When Björn walked in the front door, he heard his wife cheerfully chatting with the potential nanny. "Come meet Salomé!" she called over from the living room.

He had to bite his tongue when he saw who Tanja was interviewing. The girl's face was caked in pale foundation, she was wearing black lipstick and nail polish, and her dyed-black hair, already browning at the roots, was held in check by a half dozen bobby pins. She had several tattoos, including a raven's head on the back of her hand.

"Salomé was recommended by the Creative Nanny Agency," said Tanja. "I thought Alena might like spending time with someone who could draw pictures with her."

"What's the Creative Nanny Agency?"

"It's a program that pairs artists with kids," said Salomé. "We're like Montessori nannies."

"And the children don't find you frightening?"

"Björn!" Tanja exclaimed.

"It's okay," said Salomé. "I've never had any complaints. Anyway, I make art for a living, this is just my steady-work gig. I make things with kids and take them to museums. I know people who can get me in for free. It's pretty cool."

"Pretty cool . . ." echoed Björn in bewilderment.

Photos from Salomé's portfolio were spread out on the coffee table. Björn was confused as to why she would have brought it along. It was as if she was trying to sell her work rather than presenting herself as a babysitter. He picked up a photo of a stick figure theatrically throwing its hands up in the air. Björn read the caption aloud: *Imploring Old Man, after Rodin.*

"It's based on a detail from Rodin's *The Gates of Hell*," Salomé said proudly. "It's made entirely from matchsticks."

Björn wondered how on earth anyone could muster the patience to glue together that many matches. The result wasn't even nice to look at—it was dark and repulsive. The mouth of the small figure was open wide; for eyes, Salomé had used burnt match heads.

"It's on display at a group show right now if you want to go see it for yourself."

"I told Salomé we might check it out," said Tanja, giving Björn a look that said *just shut up and smile.* Björn wasn't sure why Tanja was so taken with someone who looked like a cartoon goth girl, but he could see that the two women were getting along—not an insignificant thing when it came to an undertaking like childcare. He glanced down at his cell phone and scrolled down a list of missed calls and new emails. One was from his PA with a departure time only a few hours away.

"I'm really sorry," he said to Salomé, "but I need to have a word with my wife." Björn looked at Tanja, nodding toward the bedroom.

"You really want some Rammstein groupie to watch our child?" Björn said after closing the door. He was struggling to keep his voice down.

"Alena has already met her. She likes her."

"Maybe she would like a normal nanny just as much?"

"She *is* normal," Tanja countered. "And if Salomé helps nurture Alena's creativity, rather than just feeding and bathing her, I'd say that's a pretty good thing."

Björn shut his eyes momentarily, then reopened them. "Okay, I will agree to give Salomé a try if you agree to not get upset at what I'm about to tell you."

"I'm already upset, but go on," she said, crossing her arms.

"I have to go to Chile . . . tonight."

Tanja rolled her eyes. "I'm sorry," Björn said. "Christophe's orders."

"If Christophe ordered you to eat your own shit, you would."

"Now hold on," Björn said, holding his hands up in protest. "It won't be like this forever. Once Nectar's IPO launches, I could stand to make millions. I could take on an advisory role and spend more time with you and Alena. But if even just one thing is off—*poof!*—there goes our chance at leaving the rat race."

"You don't get it. I don't *want* to leave the rat race, I want to get back in."

Björn shrugged his shoulders. "Whatever you say."

"Yes, whatever I say," Tanja repeated tonelessly.

At Tegel Airport, Björn met up with Armin, who was dragging a small suitcase with a broken wheel behind him. The lopsided weight caused the bag to catch on the smallest snag on the floor.

"These things are worthless without working wheels," he muttered.

While they waited for their gate to open, Armin went off in search of a luggage store. Björn facetimed Tanja to see if she had calmed down. As soon as the phone started pinging her number, he braced himself for another onslaught, but instead of a furious Tanja he found her looking worried.

"What's the matter?"

"Alena's been drawing some pictures, but they're a little—strange."

The camera moved from Tanja's face to a cushion on the sofa. Three drawings were spread out on top of it, all done in crayon. At first sight, they were the typical drawings of a five-year-old: crude flowers in a field; a crooked, two-dimensional house under the stippled rays of a rudimentary sun; a sailboat at sea. But in each one Björn could make out a mess of black scribbles invading the images.

"Can you see them?" asked Tanja.

"What is that black thing?"

Tanja moved one of the drawings closer. Within a tornado of scribbles emerged a head and disproportionately long limbs, like those of a daddy longlegs. The flowing hair was the only thing that told Björn his daughter had drawn a woman. The face was represented by a circle with two asterisks for eyes and a line for a mouth. He noticed a line dangling down from it and into the scribbling. It took him a moment to realize that the line and the scribbling were one unbroken thread, and in the woman's hand was a sewing needle.

"Who's this? Broom-Hilda the witch?"

"I don't know. It's the same image in each drawing. I watched her make the one with the boat. She had finished it and was starting on the one with the house when I left her to prepare dinner. When she came into the kitchen she was holding these drawings and she looked absolutely terrified."

"She's probably just afraid of Salomé."

"This isn't the first time she's been scared, Björn. Something is spooking her."

"Maybe check the apps on her iPad? Or her books. Or the films she is watching?"

An announcement came over the loudspeakers saying that Björn's flight was now boarding. "I have to go," he said. "But I'll be in touch after I land."

✖

Twenty-two hours later, bleary-eyed and groggy, Björn joined the arrivals queue. He handed his passport to a bored customs officer and, after a few routine questions, was waved through. In baggage claims, he and Armin pulled their suitcases off the conveyor belt and walked through customs without being bothered again.

The sky over Santiago was overcast, and a humid breeze was blowing. Armin had rented a Mercedes and was driving at top speed toward the outskirts of the city. The sedan's air-conditioning blew cold air into Björn's face. He shivered. From up on a mountaintop he saw the whole panorama: the slender, elastic high-rises stretching up in front of the snow-covered peaks like exotic plants reaching for the light, enmeshed in multilane highways reaching from the center of the city out into the plains. The Pacific was still far off, but there was salt in the air—the mild breath of the gigantic body of water that surrounded the Americas, from one hemisphere to the other.

While Armin drove east, he poured out a ceaseless flow of words, trying to lay the blame on the Chilean contractors in hopes of disguising his own failure. Björn's watch lit up: it had automatically adjusted to local time—four hours back.

In no time the car was winding its way down towards Valparaíso. Björn stared out of the window, only half taking in the town's crumbling facades, remnants of its impressive colonial architecture. The old port city's glory days were behind it now; the overwhelming majority of the three hundred thousand residents lived in colorful shacks made of wood and corrugated tin, sloping higgledy-piggledy all the way down to the Pacific.

Recently a severe earthquake had caused the walls of the city's cemetery—which clung to a steep hill—to collapse. One skeleton had hurtled down into the valley on the white marble slabs, like a cheerfully grinning skier, only coming to a standstill in front of a gas station owned by ENAP, the state oil company.

The GPS directed Armin toward the container port where a variety of commercial freight vessels and naval ships were anchored, guarded by bored-looking cadets. They pulled up in front of a squat dockside building.

"We're right on time," said Armin, trying hard to be positive.

Björn stepped out of the car and scanned the port. An aging shipping freighter bearing a German flag was moored at the wharf.

"Do you think that's one of our ships?" Björn asked, pointing at the vessel. "Weren't there supposed to be two?"

Armin popped the trunk, pretending not to have heard Björn's questions. He wheeled his case into the prefab and Björn followed behind.

They were greeted by a receptionist perched behind a rickety MDF desk. "Have a seat," she said in softly accented English. "Señors Carrera and Montes will be with you shortly."

The waiting area faced onto an aquarium in which a school of exotic fish was swimming in incessant figures of eight. Occasionally, some of the creatures nibbled at the others in their boredom. Björn recognized one as a cloudfish, which made him think of one of Alena's favorite animation films. Songs from its soundtrack were queuing up in his mind as two men in business suits entered the lobby. They introduced themselves as Carlos and Manuel from SalvoCorp, Chile's third largest logistics group. The two made an odd couple: Carlos was heavyset and sallow-faced; Manuel had an athletic build and sported a trimmed beard and horn-rimmed glasses. They led Armin and Björn to a windowless conference room cooled by a large air-conditioning unit.

"So," said Manuel smiling nervously, "welcome to Valparaíso! How was the flight? Would you like coffee or water?"

"We haven't come halfway around the world for small talk," Björn said sternly. "I'm told you are trying to sell us a derelict site as a distribution center?"

"Well, that's not quite true," said Manuel curtly. "It has not been used in some time, but it is an incredible site for your company. An abandoned mining town with fueling stations for trucks and a spacious warehouse. Even an airstrip. It's also very close to Antofagasta. We could probably get you a permanent dock so that you could ship things directly there."

Björn raised an eyebrow at Armin. "Well, if that's all true," he said, "then why are we here? Why didn't we go directly to the site?"

Carlos and Manuel looked at one another nervously. "Because there are a few, what is the word, *clunks*."

"You mean *kinks*? Like what?"

"The site is located in northern Chile, which is very hot and dusty. Some of the buildings will need to be renovated, roads will need to be repaved. It may need a new power grid."

"So then the site *is* derelict," said Björn, straining to hold back a wave of anger and frustration.

"No, it's just not ready. But we can have it redeveloped fairly quickly. Maybe not in three months, but in six or eight. Time enough to get the word out that its going to be opening. That should make your investors happy."

"That still gives us no place to put our merchandise. And while we're on that subject, where is our other ship? There are supposed to be two docked here."

Manuel leaned over to Carlos and the two began speaking in Spanish. Björn turned to Armin and whispered to him in German that they were being taken for a ride and that this entire expedition had been bullshit. If Christophe ever heard about this conversation he'd rip their heads off.

Finally, Manuel sat up and cleared his throat. Carlos smiled politely.

"The other ship refused to come down this far south, it costs them more fuel than it's worth," Manuel said. "But there's great news—we were able to convince the captain to dock at Antofagasta. In the next three months, you could easily have all of that cargo freighted to cities all over South America. And if you like, we can arrange for a plane to get you to the proposed site almost immediately. It's an easy two-hour flight."

While Björn was weighing his options, he was suddenly hit with a vicious nosebleed. He fished around in his pants pocket for a tissue, but came up empty. A crimson streak shot out of his left nostril, leaving a stain on his collar. Alarmed, Manuel directed Björn toward a bathroom. By now, thick drops were falling into Björn's cupped hand. To get the blood to clot he plugged his nose with toilet paper, then washed and dried his hands. While he waited for the bleeding to stop, he took out his phone. There was a text from Tanja: *call me asap.*

She picked up on the first ring. A somewhat distorted version of Tanja's voice was carried his way by satellite from the other side of the world.

"Alena swallowed a button."

"What kind of button?"

"A big button from my black coat, the Chanel one—it doesn't matter. A *big* fucking button. If Salomé wasn't trained in first aid, she could have choked!"

Björn pulled the bloody tissue from his nose as he spoke.

"But she's okay now?"

"We just left the emergency room to make sure she didn't swallow anything else."

Björn had never heard Tanja sound so shaken before. "Why would she even do something like that?" he asked helplessly.

"She said a woman led her into our bedroom and told her to. Alena keeps talking about this old woman. Do you think we should take her to a child psychologist?"

Björn felt dizzy and confused. He leaned his palms on the sink and saw on his watch that he had been in the bathroom for almost ten minutes. "Tanja, let me finish up my meeting and call you back."

"But I don't know if we should even go home with all this going on. What should I do?"

"Honey, I can't tell you that from all the way over here."

"Okay then," Tanja said drily. Without waiting for an answer, she hung up.

The meeting concluded soon after, but Björn was unable to reach Tanja. It was late there, he realized, and she and Alena were probably asleep.

✖

The incident was still on Björn's mind the next morning as the men rolled out onto the runway at a small airport just outside the city center. Carlos was piloting the four-seat Cessna while Manuel sat next to him, navigating.

After briefly taxiing, Carlos pulled the stick towards him and rose steeply to seven hundred feet. Björn, who was crammed into the back seat next to Armin, felt himself getting dizzy. He had slept badly and was feeling miserable. He stared fixedly out of the oval window to distract himself, but all he could see down below was desert, fringed by bare mountains to the east. Again and again, the plane lurched into air pockets, but the Chileans didn't seem bothered by it, and neither did Armin—or perhaps he didn't want to lose face any more than he already had. Manuel had put on mirrored sunglasses. Every now and then he glanced at the electronic flight plan that he had open on his iPad. Whenever they changed their course, Carlos would inform air traffic control in Antofagasta, whose crackling replies could be heard coming in over the radio.

This went on for two hours, accompanied by the ceaseless roar of the engine. Then finally Carlos pointed the nose of the airplane downward, reduced the thrust, extended the landing flaps, and touched down, bringing the Cessna to a jolting halt.

The men climbed out of the cabin and looked around. Against a dazzling panorama of glacier-encrusted mountains, the plains stretched out before them. Just a few feet in front of them lay an abandoned settlement.

Without waiting for the others, Björn headed off toward the bleak site, scowling. The remnants of whitewashed houses lined the road. Most of the roofs had caved in; the windows had been smashed;

there were broken bottles lying on the ground. A slight breeze was whirling up the dust in the alleys between the buildings.

"Miners lived in this settlement. They extracted nitrate here in the Atacama Desert," Manuel said.

During the nitrate boom 120 years before, he explained, Chile had risen to great prosperity. The substance had been in high demand all over the world for use as a fertilizer. But then German chemists had invented a cheap substitute, and the mining industry that had made Chile rich collapsed. The boom had left the country, and the army of traders, adventurers, and fortune-seekers that had inhabited this remote town had left along with it.

While Manuel expounded at length on the history of the site, Björn walked in grim silence to the main square. Apart from a dry well and a rusty silo there was nothing to see here. Armin followed a few feet behind like a beaten dog. Carlos had stayed by the plane, probably hoping to avoid the tongue-lashing that was sure to follow.

Manuel directed them into a flat warehouse at the far end of the square. Beams of sunlight poured through the long windows in the corrugated roof. Weeds grew in patches on the floor and a small feral creature darted into a corner as they walked to the center. Björn groaned.

"So this is it?" he asked. He looked furiously at Armin, then back at Manuel.

"This property has been decommissioned for a number of decades, but I can assure you that all the repairs that would have to be done are cosmetic. Just some tidying. Simple stuff."

"This place is a shithole," said Björn. "It doesn't just need tidying, it would have to be entirely rebuilt!"

Manuel began to protest. "Señor, if you could just be patient and reasonable . . ."

But Björn couldn't hold it in anymore. "No. I've been patient, but this—" he cut the air with his hand like a hatchet, "—this is a joke! The deal is off. Take us back to Santiago."

As they walked back to the airplane, Björn turned around to Armin.

"This is the worst dump I've ever seen in my life," Björn said tonelessly. "No power, no water, no infrastructure. If this isn't solved right now, you're out on your ass."

"But I told you that—"

"Tell Christophe. Good luck."

During the flight back, Björn ignored the other men and stared out the window in irritation. None of the others dared speak. Below, the endless salt flats of the Atacama sped beneath them—sand, scrubs, and stones in monotonous alternation. Björn's thoughts were somewhere else entirely; he was thinking of Christophe and how furious he would be. Armin and the Chileans had screwed up royally. Probably they'd all get fired over this debacle and he, Björn, would be exiled to some outpost—he'd get sent to build up Nectar's online business in Pakistan or something. Christophe was merciless; he didn't give a damn about people's sensitivities. While Björn was getting more and more worked up imagining increasingly dark scenarios, he spotted something on the horizon. At first it was a small dot in the distance; then it grew into a horseshoe-shaped complex of buildings. They seemed to have been concreted into the desert along the side of the Pan-American Highway. Björn leaned closer to the window, straining his eyes. He had good instincts, and they were wide awake now.

"What is that?" he asked Manuel, pointing at the low-slung buildings.

"Nothing, señor, just an internment camp from the days of the dictatorship."

"I want to have a closer look at it."

"There's no point."

"That's for me to decide!"

"We can't land here, there are still land mines buried along the road down there."

"Then fly low over it."

On Manuel's orders, Carlos reluctantly dropped down to two hundred feet and flew over the former prison two, three times. From above, they could see a power line and a cistern that both looked intact. Björn's eyes lit up. He nudged Armin.

"Well? That's *perfect*, isn't it? The trucks can park in the middle, and we'll put the warehouses on the left and right."

Armin gave him a blank look, but then quickly returned his grin, since it seemed wise to do so.

Manuel turned around to the two Germans.

"No, señor, we cannot accept this—people were tortured there. Not a good place. Carlos's brother was locked up in there in the Pinochet era."

"Is it for sale? Who owns the property?"

"Technically, we do," Manuel replied. "But trust me, this is not a place you want to buy or work in." Carlos nodded vigorously to underline the point his colleague had made.

But Björn wasn't listening. He looked down at the complex, smiling blissfully; in his head he could see the sales figures and the value of his stocks, both going up exponentially.

One full day and night later, Björn touched down in Berlin. He transitioned seamlessly from the Chilean late summer back into the Berlin winter. During his absence there had been freezing rain for two days straight. The asphalt was coated with a layer of ice an inch thick, slick as glass. In an effort to spare the environment and the state coffers, the city had neglected to salt the roads, and now the hospitals were filling up with B-list celebrities who had slipped on the ice in their high heels during the Berlinale film festival.

Björn gingerly made his way the last few feet from the taxi to his apartment, his wheeled suitcase sliding around behind him.

When he entered the apartment, expecting his daughter to come running toward him, he found the place silent. Salomé was standing out on the balcony smoking a hand-rolled cigarette. The smoke curled up from the corner of her mouth and dissipated in the icy air. Every time she lowered her hand, the glow traced a bright arc through the night sky. When she saw Björn come in she quickly put her cigarette out on the sole of her left shoe and came back inside.

"Where is everyone?" he asked.

"You just missed them. I just came back to get my purse."

She shrugged awkwardly. "Tanja thought it might be better to spend the night in a hotel."

"You're kidding. Why would she do that?"

"Well, Alena was very frightened. You heard what happened with the button, didn't you?"

"Yes, but that was two days ago. What does that have to do with them being in a hotel now?"

Salomé ran her hands through her hair nervously.

"It might all be my fault. Today, I took Alena to the Berlinische Galerie to distract her after all that excitement. I thought the little one might like it if we went and looked at some pictures. I think children can handle being exposed to grown-up art, don't you?"

"Go on."

"We went to a permanent exhibition with old photos of Berlin— factories, pubs, street scenes, that sort of thing," Salomé continued.

Björn tapped his feet impatiently. "This story better have a point."

Salomé took her tobacco pouch and squeezed it so tightly between her fingers that some loose strands fell from the flap and scattered across the floor. She bent over and started to sweep up the brown crumbs. Her face flushed.

"We walked past a portrait of an old woman. When Alena saw the picture, she stopped in front of it. She told me she recognized the lady in the picture, because she was the one who told her to swallow the button. I didn't really think anything of it at the time—I even bought a postcard of the photograph. That was stupid of me, wasn't it? But later, Alena didn't want to go back to the apartment."

Salomé shrugged helplessly.

"Don't worry, you can go now. We'll pay you for the two hours of overtime," he said distractedly, cutting her short before she could launch into further rambling explanations.

Salomé gave him a relieved look. She took her coat. "The picture really *was* a little creepy. Do you think I'm imagining it? Here, see for yourself." She pulled a flat tissue-paper envelope from her inside pocket, threw it on the table and stood waiting for his reaction. When he didn't do anything, however, she wrapped her scarf around her neck and said goodbye.

After Salomé had left, Björn called Tanja's number. She answered almost immediately.

"What?"

"Tanja, where have you been? I was worried!" he said crossly.

"Alena and I are in a hotel."

"Where?"

"In Mitte," she said.

"So when do you intend to come home?"

He could hear Alena in the background asking for him. Then Tanja spoke again. "I don't know. She keeps going on about this woman who told her to swallow the button. Today Salomé—"

"Yes, I heard. We shouldn't indulge Alena all the time—this, whatever this is, is getting ridiculous."

"Look, Björn, this isn't up for discussion. Alena nearly died. We have to play it safe."

"Well, I'm back now, and you should come back too. You can't hide in a hotel forever, that's not the way for us to sort out Alena's fears."

"What do you mean *us*? It's usually me who sorts things out. You're not even here when you *are* here."

"Listen, just come back home. I'll stay up and wait for you."

After he had hung up, Björn rooted around in the sideboard for the single malt that he had brought home from the last strategy meeting in Dublin. He felt jet lagged and sharply annoyed at his wife for making him stay up.

To take his mind off the conversation with Tanja, he reached for the envelope that Salomé had left for him.

An oval logo was printed on the flap—the logo of the museum gift shop. Björn tore the envelope open and pulled out the postcard. On the front was a portrait, reproduced in sepia. Oddly, the person in the picture wasn't looking into the camera, but at a piece of linen cloth lying in her lap. The woman was very thin, and her long, hollow-eyed face had the drawn features of a zealot. She was wearing a severe, high-collared dress, deliberately plain in a way that ran counter to what one would expect of nineteenth-century fashion, with its penchant for wide, frilly skirts. Her unnatural posture— bent over like a hook—reminded Björn involuntarily of his daughter's drawings. He went over to the sideboard with the cognac bottles and rummaged through the stack of Alena's pictures. The similarity between the childish pencil scribbles and the brownish daguerreotype was unmistakable. When Björn looked at the postcard more closely, he discovered a sewing needle in the woman's left hand, just like in Alena's picture. He turned the postcard over. There was a brief caption at the bottom: *Agnes Schildhof. Pioneer of women's rights and chairwoman of the Trade Association for Berlin Coat Seamstresses (1851–1899)*.

He pushed the postcard aside, suddenly feeling unwell. He noticed he was shivering, the first gentle paw-strokes of a fever he had picked up somewhere between the port of Valparaíso and Bar Vanilio, where he'd gone with Armin to celebrate the successful completion of their mission.

✖

"You're the ultimate wolf!"

Christophe hugged him tightly. "Woof, woof, yowl! You're the best!"

Björn disentangled himself from Christophe's claustrophobic embrace. He felt faint. They were right in the middle of Nectar's HQ, and the hubbub around them seemed dizzying and senseless.

"There's just one problem," he said hesitantly.

"Come on, man, out with it, we'll solve it."

Christophe slapped Björn on the back, flashing a huge smile at him.

"The Chilean contractors pulled out this morning."

"So what? We'll get some new ones."

"The other big company in Chile said no right away."

Christophe took a step back. He looked Björn up and down quizzically.

"You should shave, man. Are you alright?"

"Of course," Björn answered quickly, small beads of sweat forming below his hairline. He felt like he'd been caught.

"Well, so why are these people so shy to take our money? Do they think we've got syphilis or something?"

"They don't like the site we've chosen."

"And why is that?"

"It's a former labor camp. Bad things happened there."

"What, like a million years ago? Why don't they drink some ayahuasca, sweat it all out, exorcise it, that's the kind of thing they do in Chile, isn't it?"

"Sounds more like Peru."

"Whatever, man. I'm sure you'll fix it. Just take the rest of the day off, you look like shit."

Christophe gave Björn another friendly whack between the shoulder blades, then refocused his attention on the cost forecast the accounts department had prepared for the IPO.

✖

When he came home that evening, Björn found that things weren't going well. Despite how late it was, Alena was still awake, and was sitting on Tanja's lap in her nightie. She looked exhausted, her little face puffy from crying. She was clinging tightly to her mother. Salomé was there too, although her shift had long ended. She was leaning against the window fiddling with a roll-your-own. The two women seemed tense and paid no heed to Björn's presence. Only Alena seemed to register his arrival. She sighed softly, but it was unclear whether it was an expression of relief or despair.

"Everything okay?" Björn asked. He was struck by how hollow the phrase sounded, and dropped his voice to a whisper.

Tanja gathered her daughter into her arms and carried her to her bedroom like a baby.

The nanny put her unlit cigarette down on the coffee table. After a few moments, there was the sound of a music box tinkling "Frère Jacques."

Salomé anxiously drummed her fingers on the table.

"She's still afraid of that woman."

"There isn't any woman."

"Well."

Clearly there was something she wanted to tell him. She hemmed and hawed awkwardly, but finally she screwed up her courage.

"I went to the State Library yesterday . . . and I looked something up," she began haltingly. "I wanted to know who this Agnes Schildhof was that Alena recognized in the picture. She had quite an eventful life, and there were a few things that struck me as rather—uncanny. Are you interested?"

Björn narrowed his eyes, giving her a hostile look, but Salomé didn't seem to notice. She rummaged through her bag and took out an unruly stack of papers.

"I just wanted to give you a brief idea. She came from a humble background in Silesia. She eked out a living in Berlin sewing coats—hard work, and badly paid at that. Through a friend, she came into contact with a guild for seamstresses and women working as tailors. Back then it was strictly forbidden for women to be politically active . . ."

Salomé paused and looked at Björn self-consciously. "I'm not boring you, am I?"

She pointed at the photocopies. "Well, you should really see this. It's all in here:"

Schildhof was a compelling speaker and decried the conditions in which the women had to work and the bad pay. In September 1889, she was arrested and sued for lèse-majesté, which was subject to severe punishment. In prison, she went on hunger strike. Finally, the court stripped her of her legal capacity and had her committed to a mental institution, where she was force-fed with a rubber tube.

"That doesn't sound very appetizing," Björn said unenthusiastically.

He was losing his patience. He wanted to have a quiet night in, maybe watch some soccer, and then collapse into bed. Salomé's dark imagination—because how else could her fascination with these morbid stories be explained?—was the last thing he needed right now.

"And then she killed herself," the nanny added meaningfully. "She swallowed her sewing kit—needles, thimbles, all of it, and buttons, of course. A gruesome death. And you want to know what the weirdest thing is?"

Salomé lowered her voice portentously.

Björn, who was repulsed by the whole performance, scowled, but once again Salomé failed to notice.

"I'll tell you—she died right here, in the city's lunatic asylum—that's what they called it at the time. And your apartment was the morgue."

Björn was sure that Salomé had made the whole thing up. As if sensing his skepticism, she pushed the pile of photocopied documents towards him. Björn was good at reading upside down. He saw several words that looked familiar, like the name of the street he lived on. But he didn't touch the stack of papers. He now felt distinctly unwell. A prism seemed to have come between him and the world, its glass making everything seem very far away.

"Enough of this bullshit," he hissed.

Salomé stared at him, alarmed.

"I need some respite from your crap. Just *one moment* of peace."

His voice cracked. The nanny gathered her things and, without saying another word, headed for the door.

During the night, Björn's fever rose sharply. His eyes jerked and fluttered under their closed lids, chasing shadowy figures. Tanja slept on the left side of the bed. She lay motionless while Björn tossed and turned.

Björn's dreams flickered just beneath the surface of his consciousness. Amid the cacophony of fears and anxieties—missed flights, flunked exams, cliffs and abysses, hazards and humiliations—real sounds rose up through the din: his daughter, crying for help. Björn leapt out of bed and padded down the cold tiles toward Alena's bedroom. He didn't turn a light on because, in his half-asleep state, he didn't know that such a thing even existed. As he made his way down the hallway, he noticed he had begun to shiver all over.

"Daddy, hurry!" his daughter's little voice said.

Björn entered Alena's room. His senses were so addled that the scene he saw before him didn't look tangible and three-dimensional, but seemed more like a picture etched in lead. He could make out his daughter's loft bed in the shadows and, beside it, the contours of a rake-thin woman. What this person was doing there, how she had gotten into the apartment, and whether she had bad intentions, he couldn't venture to guess.

Unfazed by his presence, she was stitching strange crosses onto a white linen cloth. She had an air of austere melancholy.

She pulled the thread upward in a sweeping arc, and Björn saw that she was sewing a gown. She nodded in confirmation, her head bobbing up and down like that of a crudely carved marionette. "My burial shroud," Björn heard her think. He stepped toward the seamstress, but somehow lacked the strength to shoo her away.

"Daddy, I'm scared!" Alena said from up on her bed.

Now, without hesitation, Björn turned on the light. His senses recalibrated abruptly; his consciousness switched from sleep to waking mode. Now he saw things as they really were. He was standing in front of a wall—that's all that it was. To his left, his daughter was looking down at him with big eyes.

"She's not real," Björn said.

"I know, Daddy, but I'm still scared."

Björn lifted a hand to his forehead and felt how hot and clammy it was. He heard a noise behind him. Tanja had woken up and was standing in the doorway, rubbing her eyes sleepily.

"You look terrible," she said.

"Thanks," he replied.

The light in the desert was crystalline, the heat arid. On the horizon, giant trucks sped down the Pan-American Highway going south, but from this distance they looked like toys. Farther off, the Andes rose up to dizzying heights. A gray plume of smoke hung on one of the mountaintops.

Björn and Armin were driving down a narrow dirt road. Armin was steering the jeep with great care, because diamond-shaped signs on his right reminded them of the land mines that lay buried in the desert beyond the road.

Björn looked out the window anxiously. "A bit scary, isn't it?"

"It is what it is," Armin replied somewhat peevishly.

They passed over a hump in the road and a large building complex loomed up before them. The cell blocks were long and low-slung. It looked completely abandoned. Along the length of the squat rectangle, there were windows lined with blue-gray bars, the paint flaking off them.

"We're working with a new logistics company. As you know, the Chileans refused to work here," Armin said, with the hint of an unspoken accusation.

He parked the car in front of a massive gate that had originally been placed there to prevent attempted breakouts. As Björn got out the passenger door, a dust devil, as tall as he was, swept in and completely blinded him for several seconds. He shielded his eyes. Beside him, Armin muttered an incomprehensible curse that culminated in a coughing fit. Then the apparition was past. The two men brushed sand—half of it fine-grained salt—off their clothes.

Björn regretted having left his long-sleeved shirt in his suitcase. The sun was beating down on them; it felt as if it was actually piercing his skin.

As he and Armin headed towards the horseshoe-shaped complex, a squat man with Native American facial features came over to them and greeted them with a broad grin.

"That's Edmundo. He's our new site manager." Edmundo wedged the clipboard he'd been holding under his arm and gave Björn a firm handshake. A long stream of words in Spanish—incomprehensible to Björn—came pouring out of his mouth.

"He's from Peru. All the people we have working for us here are: the truckers, the stock-pickers—the whole lot of them," Armin said, and added proudly, "They're only costing us a fraction of what the Chileans were asking."

Edmundo grabbed Björn by the arm and pulled him toward the low building that marked the left perimeter of the complex. From the sweltering courtyard they came into the no-less-stifling heat of the former cell block. The partition walls had been knocked out and at right angles to the small, barred windows they had put up metal shelves stacked with cardboard boxes. Women with notepads were scurrying among the shelves and pulling the heavy boxes, containing domestic appliances from various manufacturers, onto stock trolleys. Further back, other women were packaging and labeling the products that had been selected.

One woman was sitting exhausted in a corner, fanning herself with a piece of paper. Edmundo shook her roughly. Then he showed the two Germans his workstation: an antiquated computer terminal which was ceaselessly spitting out new orders as they were being placed online. A slow fan whirred overhead, churning the sticky air.

Björn loosened his tie. "Is there no air-conditioning in here?"

Armin gave him a baffled look.

"Do you know what it would cost to keep this kind of space cool? We'd need to have our own generator!"

Gesturing toward the workers, Björn asked, "Where have you put these women up?"

"Diagonally across, in Block B."

After their brief tour, Björn and Armin retreated into the rental car and turned the fan up to full blast.

"You know, I'm not so sure about this," Björn mumbled after a while.

"About what?" Armin asked, annoyed.

"About everything."

Armin gave Björn a blank look, but Björn kept his eyes trained on the shimmering desert outside.

IFRIT

I HAD STARTED DOING YOGA because I was having problems with my shoulder. My ex had recommended I go to Rocket's classes. "They're very effective, but they're not for the fainthearted," she'd warned. And indeed, nothing about these evening sessions resembled run-of-the-mill yoga. It felt more like a cult without a doctrine, and Rocket was our undisputed leader. In the first class, Rocket had sat down on my chest with no prior warning and pulled on my left arm. There was a cracking sound somewhere above my collarbone, in a place I hadn't known existed. After that I had complete movement of my shoulder again. Over the next few days, the pain that had accompanied me for months gradually subsided. "Trust yourself," Rocket had said.

The classes took place in the early evening and I never dared come late, not wanting to offend Rocket. The master himself was last to arrive. He had thick white hair which he gathered into a whip-like plait. Watery blue eyes peered out from beneath bushy eyebrows and fixed us disciples with their stare. His hawk's nose and angular chin completed the air of authority. Although there was little about Rocket's squat, stocky physique that could be called handsome, women seemed to love his confident manner. Folding his hands in front of him, he would intone: "*Om shanti om*, peace be with you," in the mishmash of languages that he'd gotten used to speaking during his time in India.

We'd begin harmlessly enough with breathing exercises, closely monitored by Rocket's watchful eye. We sat close together under neon tube lights. Usually we'd start cross-legged with the *ujjayi* breath, which involves producing an aspirate sound. He would explain that the life energy—known in yogic philosophy as *prana*—would be able to flow through our veins more freely now. We would conclude this part of the practice with *kapalabhati*, the forceful exhalations of the skull-shining breath.

Under his tutelage, people who would never have expected themselves to be capable of such a thing would end up doing a headstand, while others who couldn't so much as carry a shopping bag home from the grocery store would assume the flying pigeon pose, where the body weight rests entirely on the arms. When one of us failed to execute a pose to his satisfaction, he would show little mercy in helping us along. His big hands would use just enough force to stretch us to our limits.

Rocket's renown reached far beyond the yoga scene. He was a Kreuzberg icon: first-generation squatter, Ganges pilgrim, activist. In 1981, he and his art collective called *Fliegenpilz* ("Fly Agaric") had stolen the May tree from in front of the Christian Social Union's party headquarters in Munich and driven it all the way to Checkpoint Charlie on the roof of his VW van. He'd spent the seventies partly in an ashram and partly on the front lines of the squatting movement's battles in Berlin. He had to appear in court multiple times: twice for inciting public disturbance (convicted), three times for serious breach of the peace (convicted), and once for aiding and abetting a terrorist organization (acquitted).

When in 1984 the city offered to legalize the apartment on Bergmannstrasse that he had occupied with his girlfriend Dany and his friend Rabbit-Kalle, he agreed. Other squatters who made these kinds of deals were reviled by the whole community. But nothing could sully Rocket's reputation; he was untouchable. In the noughties, he and his partner had bought the apartment, along with a smaller unit on the floor below.

After one yoga class, Rocket mentioned offhandedly that the smaller apartment would become available at the end of the month. Since I was looking for a place I went up to him. "Great—we're looking for someone who'll be a good fit with us. Stop by tomorrow, we'll all be making the decision together—the whole collective."

I learned the next day that the collective consisted of Rocket, Dany, who seemed withdrawn and gray, his second partner Nina—who had multiple piercings and was at least thirty years younger—and Rabbit-Kalle, a scruffy guy in his late fifties with a beard who spoke in a near-unintelligible mumble. We all sat down together in the kitchen next to the yoga studio, drinking herbal tea. I did my best to cover up the fact that I'm a Gen Y-er whose lifestyle these people would surely despise. My hero was Mark Zuckerberg, whom I also resembled physically. My goals in life were: to earn a good living and start a family at some point—but not too soon. I was barely interested in politics and had never rebelled against anything. I kept silent about all of this and instead talked about the small ice-cream factory my buddy Max and I were busy getting off the ground. We planned to work only with fair-trade ingredients, since that was currently in high demand. Rocket nodded appreciatively. When the others saw that he seemed to be happy, they nodded too. "I feel good vibes," Rocket said and looked around him. "Nina will show you the apartment and then you can make up your mind."

He reached into his half-unbuttoned linen shirt and pulled out a keychain that hung from a cord around his neck. Nina jumped up and took it from him. She gestured for me to follow her.

We went down to the floor below. The apartment was flooded with milky winter light. Rocket had just stripped the hardwood floor, and the entryway smelled of varnish. Nina kicked her flats into a corner and walked barefoot on the pale floorboards. "It feels sooo nice on your feet," she said. Silver bracelets dangled around her slender ankles. She hop-skipped into the living room. Nina was older than me, but she seemed radiant, fit, and overflowing with energy. Her blonde hair was held back by a pink bandana. She exuded the kind of joie de vivre whose upper ranges verge on hysteria.

"Did you just get back from vacation?" I asked, gesturing at her lower arm, which was tanned a rich brown like the rest of her body. "Oh no, that's from the summer. Kreuzberg-by-the-Sea," she replied, gesturing vaguely in the direction of Viktoriapark. We went into the living room, which looked out onto the quiet stretch of Bergmannstrasse that runs north from Marheinekeplatz. I slowly spun around. There was well-preserved molding on the ceiling.

We continued our tour. My square table would fit perfectly in the kitchen. The bedroom was very small, but then I'd be asleep in there anyway, so what did it matter? The apartment wasn't exactly cheap, but the rent was much less than what some shysters were asking. "I like it," I said, my voice echoing in the empty space. "I'll take it if you guys will give it to me."

"Oh, I'd be so happy to have you," Nina said and threw her arms around me. I was taken aback by this effusive display of emotion, but I let it wash over me. Nina drew back and smiled at me. "Dany knew straightaway that you were the one. She can see people's auras, and she told us yours is big and blue on the inside—that's your inner peace—and orange on the outside—that's your strength."

In spite of this good omen, Rocket's collective made me wait for three days before summoning me again. Again it was Nina who had been chosen to meet me, this time to convey the group's decision. She gave me the good news on the threshold of my new apartment: "Congratulations, we've made the unanimous decision to accept you as our new tenant," she said rather formally. I noticed that Nina seemed more self-conscious than the first time we had met. "I wish I could give you the key right now, but you have to transfer the deposit first. Art Collective Fliegenpilz e.V. at the Volksbank Berlin."

"Of course," I said.

She fidgeted with her nose ring absentmindedly.

"You'll see, we're easy to get along with. I know may be a little unusual—me and Rocket, and Dany being part of it too. You see, the two of them have been together for so long, they're practically an old married couple . . ."

There were footsteps on the stairs. Nina's voice trailed off. "But, whatever," she added, staring off fixedly into the middle distance.

She turned around abruptly and yelled something at Rocket, who was just heading downstairs, dressed in mechanic's overalls with an axe slung over his shoulder. I waved at him. Rocket grinned at me, revealing a perfect row of ivory-colored veneers.

"Welcome, my brother. You won't regret it." He excused himself, saying he had to go chop wood for the stove and that Nina would help me deal with "the usual nonsense." As it turned out, he was referring to the slew of formalities that renting an apartment involves: producing a copy of your credit report, proof of income, and so on.

A week later, I showed up with a transporter van, two helpers, and fifteen boxes.

Not long after I moved in, I invited Max over, the buddy who was my business partner in the ice-cream venture. We ended up getting shit-faced and talking about our exes. Max's relationship had lasted all of two weeks. Sophie and I had been together for a year. In the beginning she had said to me, "You're a mystery to me—like a prism that refracts the light, and you never get to see what's inside it." Twelve months later, she had refined this point of view: "You're an arrogant asshole."

Max erupted in raucous laughter. "You have to give it to her—she's got a point."

I wanted to come back with some smart-ass reply, but I was much too drunk. Instead I got up, swaying on my feet, to punch him in the face. In the fraction of a second in which I drew back my arm, the kitchen door slammed shut and broke the ring finger of my right hand, which I'd been using to lean against the doorframe. The pain was so excruciating that there was no doubt about it: the bone had snapped in two. At the Urban Hospital, my self-diagnosis was promptly confirmed, and the finger was put in a cast. They told me that, since it was a clean fracture, I could expect it to heal relatively fast.

Max made some crack about God's wrath having come down on me. I swallowed one thousand milligrams of ibuprofen and bit my tongue so as not to give him the added satisfaction of rising to his mockery.

Sometime later, I was walking into the kitchen in my silk bathrobe (a gift from my ex) to make some coffee. Since I was still a little drowsy and am sensitive in the mornings due to low blood pressure, I was leaning against the edge of the doorframe with my good hand. Suddenly the hinges squealed. I jerked back. This reflex was my salvation, because a fraction of a second later the door again banged shut. This time I decided to get to the bottom of the matter. At first I suspected a draft, but all the windows were closed. I opened the door and eyed it suspiciously. Then I examined the hinges, but I couldn't see anything out of the ordinary. Finally I got a barbell and leaned it against the door. But the barbell toppled over and the door slammed shut again. After two days I got fed up with the situation and decided to ask Rocket, whom the collective had decided was to act as my landlord, for help.

I found him in the courtyard, where he was engaged in his favorite pastime: chopping wood. It was a gray December day, and Berlin was bitterly cold. In spite of the freezing temperature,

Rocket was dressed in just jeans and an old Metallica t-shirt. His burly body was steaming in the winter air.

A little off to the side, Rabbit-Kalle was sitting on an upturned paint can, a bottle of beer in his hand. Rocket went about his work in a series of practiced gestures. He would drive the blade into the wood with a calculated movement. Then he would swing the axe, with the log attached, high over his head and bring it down onto a tree trunk. The log would split with a loud crack. All this took place without any discernible effort on his part. When he saw me coming into the cramped courtyard, he paused. The wintry half light fell slantwise onto his face. His eyes disappeared underneath his bushy eyebrows.

"You weren't at yoga, my brother," he said, doing his best to sound casual.

"You weren't there," Rabbit-Kalle echoed in confirmation from over in the corner.

I held up my cast. "I can't."

I told them how my accident had transpired, and that I hadn't managed to find the cause of the problem.

"Hang on, I'll be right there," Rocket said. "We'll get it sorted."

His voice had the kind of deep timbre that creates an air of authority and confidence. I nodded gratefully and let him get on with his chopping. As I walked through the back door into the house, I heard the *thwack!* of the axe splitting a branch in two.

Half an hour later, my doorbell rang. Rocket had put on a boiler suit and was carrying a toolbox. I showed him the kitchen door. He lifted it out of the doorframe with an effortless motion, rubbed some old varnish off the hinges and carefully oiled them.

"So far so good," he said with satisfaction.

Then he carefully hung the door back in place and opened and closed it a few times. Rocket scratched his head. "Hmm—there are no springs in there." He nudged the door and let it swing open.

"Sometimes this sort of thing is due to bad karma, my friend, and there's no external cause."

"Really?" I asked, baffled.

He opened the toolbox and pulled out a small rubber clip which he pushed over the edge of the door, just above the door handle.

"At least now it won't slam shut again."

He gave me a firm pat on the shoulder to signal that I was no longer to worry. I felt affirmed in my masculinity by the decisive gesture. We shook hands. "See you later, alligator," he said.

While the problem with the door had been fixed, there was worse trouble to come. I'm fortunate to be a deep, healthy sleeper. But one night I jolted awake at 3:00 a.m. feeling incredibly faint. For a moment I was wondering whether I was perhaps having some kind of attack. My head was spinning and I thought I might have to vomit. I'd gone to yoga the night before and felt just fine, so this was doubly mystifying. I sat up, my mind racing, trying to work out what was going on—food poisoning, nervous breakdown, an aneurysm? Suddenly I smelled something nasty—the sulfurous odor of escaping gas. I acted immediately. Without thinking I threw the window open and sucked in the cold night air. Then I went into the kitchen, where the gas stove was. I found the back burner hissing audibly and the knob turned up all the way. Since there was no one in the apartment apart from me and the door was locked from the inside, I had to have turned the gas on myself. But I couldn't recall anything of the sort; I hadn't even cooked the night before. I'm not inclined to paranoia, but this was highly peculiar. I wished there were someone to talk to about it, but Max would have laughed in my face, Sophie had split, and my parents would have worried.

Max and his buddy Steffen had talked me into coming along to the Christmas market in Marienheide, all the way in southwest Berlin, out in the suburbs. They wanted to do their Christmas shopping and then have some mulled wine. After the previous night's scare I didn't really feel up for anything, but I ended up getting in Steffen's car after all.

We parked in the back of Lehmann's farm shop. An older lady—

drunk, and leaning on her surly-looking daughter for support—elbowed her way past me. Behind them, someone loudly shouted "Anne!" but they didn't respond.

An illuminated plastic star with a comet's tail dangled over the end of the alley. Wet snow was coming down from the dark sky and sticking to the soles of my Timberlands.

When we stepped out onto the packed town square, a children's choir, all dressed up as angels, was performing out in front of the apse of the floodlit fieldstone church. The air smelled of horse dung, resin, and roasted almonds. The traditional Christmas pyramids from the Ore Mountain region were spinning in the first stall like stacked wedding cakes, the rotor on top driven by the warm air from the lit candles that ringed the tiered nativity scenes. I pushed my way through the crowd. The choir launched into a slightly off-key rendition of *"Es kommt ein Schiff geladen"* ("There Comes a Ship A-Laden"), followed by polite applause from the surrounding crowd. Someone was taking pictures of the hurly-burly with the flash on. By the volunteer firefighter stall, I realized I had lost Max and Steffen. Contrary to their previously stated intentions, they had headed straight for a mulled-wine stand and were gathered around a steaming copper cauldron with other like-minded visitors. They beckoned me over, but I pretended not to see them. I preferred to drift through the narrow lanes between the stalls on my own in the anonymous crowd.

After a quarter of an hour, I got to the eastern exit of the market, which came out onto a former country estate. It was slightly less crowded here, and the stalls were more reminiscent of a flea market than a commercial event. A little farther off, three brindle ponies were eating hay from a zinc trough. Right next to them a woman was selling incense and Tibetan bowls. When she brushed her gray hair from her forehead, I realized it was Rocket's girlfriend, Dany.

"Hey, how's it going?" I asked.

She looked at me in surprise.

"Oh, it's you. Not so good."

"Not enough sales?"

"It's never enough. I don't get a pension. I'm broke."

She rubbed her hands together, which were protected from the cold by knitted fingerless gloves. I was taken aback by the vehemence of her reply.

"What about the yoga school?"

"Pffft. It's the collective's. Rocket's organization. I get nothing from it."

She told me about herself and her life on Bergmannstrasse. At some point I began to understand that she felt like nothing more than a guest in Rocket's apartment at this point.

"It's not just us anymore, now that Nina's there. That free love stuff sounded good when I was twenty. At sixty, I'm too old for all that. Call me a square if you want. You know, the apartment's actually mine—I bought it with my pop's money when he died. But I put it in the collective's name—in return for shrooms, pah!"

She twisted her mouth as if she'd swallowed something bitter.

"Meditation can't buy you nothing, you know?"

"But what about Rocket? Surely he helps you?"

"He gets pissed when I ask for money. You know, we never married. If we were forced to settle down properly, just the two of us, he'd still never marry me. He thinks we gotta keep that *freedom*. Pah—freedom! Fine, I don't need him to take care of me. I have my €404 a month welfare check."

She fell silent and looked at her bluish fingertips. She realized she had overwhelmed me with her outburst—what was I supposed to say to all that?

"How's yourself? You don't look so good either," she said after a moment, surveying me from head to toe. "What's up with your aura?"

I shrugged my shoulders.

"Do I even have one?"

"Course you do—we all do. Yours is purple and all shriveled up."

Suddenly I felt emboldened. Since Dany had shared her sorrows with me, I could be open with her too. I told her about my failed relationship, about how lonely I'd been feeling and the near catastrophe with the stove. She listened to me attentively.

"I can tell you, the thing with your girl is normal, that happens to all of us. But the thing with your apartment is . . . troubling," she said darkly.

"Why is that stuff happening? Are there rats under the floorboards that are tinkering with my stove?"

Dany picked up on my sarcasm and looked at me seriously.

"It's not that simple."

Our conversation was briefly interrupted. I had to step aside as three scraggly ponies were led past me.

"How do you mean?" I asked when the procession had moved on.

"Well—the apartment has bad karma, that's the problem. Why don't you talk to the people who lived there before—they can tell you why."

In that moment, I heard someone calling my name loudly. It was Steffen, slightly drunk, with Max trailing behind him. He beckoned me over.

"There you are!" they called in unison. I realized there was no getting away from the two of them, so I nodded at Dany and indicated to her that I'd like to continue the conversation some other time. She looked up at me with a mixture of worry, curiosity, and sympathy.

When I had gotten back to the square outside the church, arm in arm with the guys, I turned back toward her one more time. She was still looking at me, squinting like nearsighted people do.

The following night, I dreamt that I was in Saudi Arabia and was about to be executed. I had been instructed to lay my neck on a curved blade. The executioner was going to approach from the side and hit it with a large wooden mallet to separate my head from my body. I was lying shackled in my cell. Rabbit-Kalle came in and put an executioner's hood over his head. I cried out in fear, because I knew he would botch the whole thing. He was too drunk to aim accurately, and he wasn't strong enough to swing the hammer with enough force. When I stepped out onto the square where the executions took place, my worst fears were confirmed. Even the blade looked dull and rusty. I nevertheless tried to position my head as best I could to make Rabbit-Kalle's job easier. The crowd was jeering all around us. Suddenly everything seemed bright and overexposed. The executioner proudly drummed on his chest. He took the mallet and swung it high in the air before striking.

I sat up and calmly turned on the light. The back of my head was hurting. I touched my hair and felt a wet spot; there was a small amount of blood on my fingertips. I looked around in confusion. I didn't know what I could have hit myself on; the bed didn't have any posts. I stumbled to the bathroom and got two pieces of Kleenex, which I pressed against the back of my head until the small wound had congealed.

The next day I had to go to the hardware store on Hermannplatz to buy the large tubs that Max and I needed to make our ice cream. We wanted to start the pilot phase in February with two centrifuges. We were planning to supply our organic ice-cream flavors to a dozen ice-cream parlors and restaurants in the city. The preparations were in full swing. Max wanted to come get me around three in a pickup truck and drive me and my purchases to the factory space we had rented on Baumschulenweg. I was running a little late and hurried across Kottbusser Damm. As I was scanning the cars that were just coming around the corner, I spotted two familiar faces across the street. In a small town, the couple, who were holding hands, would have caught people's attention, but here in Berlin-Neukölln nobody noticed them. Rocket was walking on the right, as always seemingly oblivious to the cold, wearing jeans, an orange turtleneck, and a beret. His face seemed as if carved out of wood, full of notches and hard edges. His white ponytail swung from the back of his head. Nina had her arm linked through his. She was positively glowing. Her hair was down; her cheeks were red and her lips glistened with a subtle lip gloss. Next to the stocky man more than twice her age, Nina seemed even more youthful and enchanting. When they reached the large double doors of the Karstadt department store, she unbuttoned her coat. I spotted a small bump—most likely she was pregnant.

The next morning, I had an appointment with the owner of a restaurant in Schöneberg. I brought ten different kinds of ice cream with me in a cooler. He insisted that I try all of the flavors with him, including the exotic combinations we had just come up with. Max and I had gone out on the town the night before; I was feeling queasy and my desire to partake of plantain ice cream with green pepper was, accordingly, low. I had no choice, however; I emptied one paper cup after another, waxing lyrical about the fresh and natural flavors of my offerings. When, around 2:00 p.m., we finally reached a deal, I drove straight home. By then I felt like throwing up. As I was lying there in bed the apartment began to seem sinister and threatening to me. I discovered a crack in the ceiling above me and started to become convinced that at any moment a big chunk of stucco was going to come crashing down, straight onto my face. It was a ludicrous notion, but I was completely sure of it. Even the walls had it in for me; the power cables were buzzing inside the plaster like malevolent insects. I knew I would find no peace here.

I decided to go for a walk around Chamissoplatz. Unfortunately, however, it turned out that the entire block was closed for filming. There were big trucks parked everywhere that the passersby were having to squeeze past. Amid all the production managers darting around with headsets on, I spotted Dany making her way through the cable reels and generators with two heavy canvas bags. When she saw me, she put down her shopping and started rummaging in her purse.

"I wanted to give you this."

She pressed a piece of gray recycled paper into my hand. The note said, in careful schoolgirl cursive, "Demircan Karabulut," followed by a phone number.

"Who's that?"

"He used to live in your apartment. Why don't you give him a call?" She looked at me conspiratorially. "Trust me, it'll be worth your while."

She gathered her bags and gave me a friendly nod before disappearing back into the hubbub.

For two days I carried the note around in my coat pocket. I didn't touch it; I wanted to ignore it. But some things come creeping back up to the surface even when you try to suppress them. Finally I cracked and dialed the number.

"Karabulut," a hoarse male voice said.

"I'm the current tenant of the apartment you used to live in on Bergmannstrasse. Dany gave me your number."

The person on the other end of the line muttered something that didn't sound friendly.

His irritable tone threw me off. I stammered incoherently, trying to put into words something that I didn't even comprehend myself: "I've had so much trouble since moving in, first with the door, then something hit me at night and I nearly got gassed by the stove . . ."

I trailed off. Even though my attempt at explaining my predicament had been rather pathetic, Karabulut did seem to understand that I was having problems with his former apartment and wanted to ask his advice.

"No talking now," he said. "I go back to work now. Come see me Friday, four o'clock. Buschkrugallee, number 117." His voice sounded marginally more friendly now. I thanked him profusely—maybe a little too profusely. When I hung up, I felt embarrassed.

For a moment, I considered canceling the meeting straightaway, but I didn't have the courage to call a second time.

As I headed southeast from the Grenzallee U-Bahn station toward Buschkrugallee, I regretted not taking a taxi. A steady drizzle of sleet was chilling me to the bone. I'd put on the wrong jacket; the blue one without a hood instead of my waterproof, duck-down puffer jacket. The walk was about three times farther than I had estimated, and ten times as depressing. The buildings that lined these streets had been thrown up no less haphazardly than their precursors had been bombed flat in the war. All the city fathers had cared about had been cramming as many people as possible into these grim tower blocks. A few structures from the sixties looked like failed attempts at Bauhaus—they aped the style's forms but had no life to them. To my left, several lanes of cars hurried from one red light to the next; every now and then a horn would blare if someone felt things weren't moving fast enough. Just past an especially ugly prefab—a job center—I found number 117. A honeycomb of dead-looking windows faced out from a gray-beige concrete shell onto the tangle of traffic that came heedlessly barreling past on its way out of the city.

There was a Vietnamese takeout on the ground floor of the building; two red vinyl bar stools were crammed into the narrow space. The stench of rancid peanut oil came wafting out. I spotted Karabulut's nameplate and rang the doorbell firmly. A crackling barrage of sound came bursting out of the intercom that could have been any number of things—spontaneous shouts of joy, a curse, a dog barking—but not words in any human language. Then the buzzer sounded, and I found myself in the stairwell.

Karabulut was waiting for me in his doorway. To my relief, he seemed more agreeable than I'd imagined. He was somewhere between sixty and seventy and was wearing a gray suit with suspenders and a yellow sweater, a gaudy watch on his wrist. Despite his white stubble and large nose, his facial features were soft—the face of a responsible family man.

He invited me into his apartment, which was small and seemed very tidy. Karabulut's wife Aynur took my coat. She seemed younger and more fashion-conscious than her husband. Where he seemed phlegmatic, she came across as cheerful and alert. She wore an elegant headscarf pushed far back on her head, and a flatteringly cut dress. We went into the tiny, overheated living room. I sat down on the brown sofa pushed up against the front wall. I had almost failed to notice my host's mother. She was sitting across from me by the radiator, still as a statue, staring into nothingness. She was dressed in all black, from her headscarf down to her ankle-length skirt. Her face was webbed with small wrinkles. Her eyes were blue-gray and murky. "My mother is blind," Karabulut said.

I greeted the old lady, but she didn't respond. There was a brief, uncomfortable silence. Maybe she didn't want to talk to me, or maybe she had dementia. Thankfully, Karabulut's wife came in just then with a round tray. She offered me a glass of black tea, which I gratefully accepted. When I took a sip, I scalded my tongue. The tea was hot, strong, and very sweet.

"So, how I can help you?" Karabulut asked.

"Well . . . six weeks ago I moved into your old apartment on Bergmannstrasse. Since then a number of strange things have happened—accidents, but that's not all."

I told him the whole story, showed him my broken finger, and didn't leave out the nightmare either. Karabulut listened attentively. When I had finished, he leaned in close to me.

"And what would you like that I say to this?" he asked.

"Have you ever noticed anything about the apartment? Something that could explain these incidents somehow?"

Karabulut scowled.

"Apartment was good, just house bad. Always trouble, noise, you know? Upstairs, the yoga, Fliegenpilz—terrible!"

"What was it that bothered you?"

"Back in eighties, they squatted apartment. All illegal, and they living like filthy pigs. One time I was standing in the courtyard with my father. Suddenly rain comes falling down. But it wasn't rain. They were pissing out of window! All drugged up, they pissing, and I downstairs with two children and parents! Always trouble, house searches upstairs, police, and I working, you understand? Shifts at Bahlsen. Cookie factory. Up 4:00 a.m. All night long noise, music. When I say *quiet!* they no listen, they just laugh."

Karabulut had talked himself into a fury. His wife put a calming hand on his shoulder, but he turned away from her.

"I very rarely hear any noise from upstairs," I said, in an attempt to rebalance the scales. Unfortunately, my interjection had the opposite effect.

"You know what they say?" Karabulut shouted, beside himself with anger now. "They say *we* too noisy with family, when they upstairs do meditation. That's what he said to me, before he throw me out!"

"Who, Rocket?"

The mention of his name seemed to kindle a white-hot hatred in Karabulut. The more emotional he became, the worse his German got.

"I hope that Rocket drop dead!" he shouted angrily. "Right after he buy rent go up, up, up! My mother no pension, understand? My family living there since 1971—parents, us, our children. And then he say: too loud, not enough rent, no disturb meditation!"

Karabulut slumped back in his seat. His lips had turned purple. For a moment, I thought he'd had a heart attack.

Aynur Karabulut cleared her throat. "Would you like some more tea?"

Her voice rang through the silence. I held up my glass.

"But you don't remember there being anything . . . strange about the apartment?" I asked, lowering my voice so as not to wind him up even more.

Karabulut narrowed his eyes. "No, I remember nothing like that."

In spite of my burned tongue, I tried to gulp down my hot tea as quickly as I could.

"I should get going. Thank you for going out of your way."

As I was heading for the door, I heard the old blind woman saying something in Turkish behind me. Her harsh voice reminded me of the cawing rooks that gather on the Tempelhofer Feld this time of year. Her empty eyes were upturned toward the ceiling and, in the light of the floor lamp, had a slightly blue sheen. The old woman's hands were clawed tightly onto the armrests of her chair, as if she were trying to keep the earth from spinning wildly off into the universe.

"Wait!" Karabulut said in my direction. He bent down to his mother and listened to what she had to say, furrowing his brow in concentration. The exchange between them, while I stood waiting by the doorway with my jacket in my hand, was brief and urgent. After a minute or so the old woman fell silent. Her hands unclenched, and she sank back into the glazed-over, vacant state that I had first found her in. Karabulut spoke into the silence.

"My mother says you have problem because apartment not empty yet. Something stayed. Something is now very angry because we not there and no respect."

"What do you mean, *something*?" I asked, confused.

"We lived there long time, on Bergmannstrasse," he replied evasively.

"The whole town that my husband is from in Anatolia moved into Bergmannstrasse in the sixties. They've all had to leave Kreuzberg now—it's become too expensive," his wife added.

The couple exchanged a few words in Turkish.

"Any trash has disappeared in the apartment?" Karabulut asked.

"You mean household waste? Not that I know of," I replied, confused.

"Don't worry," Aynur said. "We'll send someone over who'll take care of the problem."

"Who exactly do you want to send over?" I asked, but there was no reply. Karabulut gently steered me toward the front door. Aynur shrugged her shoulders. With the utmost politeness I was maneuvered into the stairwell. Karabulut mumbled something—a goodbye or a brief word of encouragement, I guessed—before closing the door behind me. I stared, perplexed, at the glass spyhole. I thought I could see Karabulut's eye staring back at me. I made a point of leisurely putting my jacket on and headed back home.

As my finger was beginning to heal now, my doctor had, with some cautions, given me permission to go back to doing yoga. I was glad about that—not so much because I had missed the practice but because I was hoping to fill up one or two empty evenings by going. During my first session after the forced break I noticed that, in my absence, the exercises had become even more extreme. Sometimes I had the impression Rocket actually wanted us to sprain our joints. The master himself seemed agitated and irritable. While we were doing the locust, he strode down the rows of yoga mats, nervously snapping his fingers. When he had reached the back of the room, he came upon Dany. Something about the way she was doing the posture seemed to be bothering him. He impatiently grabbed her right shoulder and wrenched it back. Dany let out a clearly audible moan.

"Ow, you're hurting me!"

"You're not doing it right. You need to open the chakra!"

He pulled on her shoulder once again, even harder this time. Dany whimpered. Several of the other students looked over at Rocket in irritation. One woman who was wearing dental braces and looked kind of prim spoke up on our behalf.

"Hey, leave her alone."

For a moment, a haunted silence came over the group. No one dared speak. The woman with the braces looked over at Rocket angrily. At first it seemed like he was going to ignore her comment. Then he abruptly let go of Dany and barked, "Alright, folks, we're doing the warrior pose, let's go!"

I didn't see Dany again that evening. She probably left the studio early, slipping out through the door that led to Rocket's apartment.

One afternoon, my door buzzer went off without warning. I would normally only answer the door when I was expecting a guest, but whoever it was held down the button until I gave in and opened up. With the impersonal efficiency of paramedics, two Turkish men, dressed in long, flowing white robes, came sweeping into my apartment. The older of the two was bald; his hands were carefully manicured and there was a deep frown line on his forehead. The other, who seemed to be his assistant, was rake thin and wore the cheap glasses of someone who only has public health insurance. He dragged in a yellow suitcase, heavy metal objects clanking around in it as he walked. The two men headed straight for the living room. The bald one turned around and said over his shoulder that Karabulut had sent him. He had an air of cool authority that made me feel unsure of myself. He gestured to his helper, who immediately went off and got a chair from the kitchen and placed it in the exact center of the room. He gestured for me to have a seat.

"What exactly are you planning on doing?" I asked nervously as I sat down.

Rolling up his sleeves, the bald man eyed me skeptically. His gaze told me that he considered talking to me to be a waste of his time, but that he would do so anyway out of professional courtesy.

"You have a problem with an ifrit. We will force him to retreat back into the earth."

"What's an ifrit?" I asked, but the helper, who was flipping open the suitcase, put his index finger to his lips to bid me be silent. Then he handed his master various objects: a silver bowl, a paper bag, a lighter. The bald man took an amber-colored substance out of the bag, poured it into the bowl, and lit it. Meanwhile, the other man pulled a double-edged dagger out of the suitcase and carefully placed it on a tray next to him. I watched these preparations nervously out of the corner of my eye. The older man lifted the bowl to his chest and began to rotate it clockwise, reciting a chant—probably a passage from the Koran. Smoke ribboned up from the gleaming amber granules and the room filled with the scent of incense. The tiny particles tickled my throat, but I suppressed the urge to cough. The bald man walked over to each of the four corners of the room. Each time, he would pause there for a moment and bark a harsh command at something invisible.

The thin man had produced another item from the suitcase. He was standing behind me so I couldn't see what it was, but it was easy to figure out from the sound—a tambourine, which he was tapping in the rhythm of a heartbeat. At the same time, the master's singing and shouted commands started to become more urgent. In the midst of this mounting crescendo, the doorbell once again rang loudly. The helper put down his instrument and walked into the hallway to open up. I heard a female voice.

One of the wonders of our memory is that entire years of our lives sink into its depths without a trace, while significant moments that in reality only lasted the blink of an eye are enlarged, as if under a magnifying glass.

There was murmuring in the hallway; something was passed from hand to hand, and then the door closed again. The helper came back into the living room and handed his master a live black rooster. The animal was flailing its head wildly, its comb flapping from side to side. The bird was so keenly aware of the exceptional situation it found itself in that it didn't make a sound; I suppose it didn't want to draw attention to itself. It wasn't struggling either, like panicked chickens normally do. Its eyes, however, bulged hideously out of its ugly, plum-sized head.

The thin man picked up his tambourine and began to shake it wildly, the jangles rattling loudly. Meanwhile his master had the rooster clenched under his arm so that it couldn't flap its wings. Without much ado, he now took the silver dagger and sliced the creature's head clean off. It hit the floorboards with a slap. The rooster's talons twitched for a moment; then its feathered body ceased all further activity. Vivid red blood came spurting out of the stump of its neck, which the master now aimed directly at me. A fountain of spray hit me straight in the face. As I turned away, I felt its warmth splashing on my skin. I closed my eyes reflexively, but I seemed to have gotten some in them anyway, because I felt an intense burning sensation. In my blindness I could feel the hot liquid soaking through my t-shirt; now the bald man was aiming at my chest. I leapt to my feet and cried out—I don't remember what. At the same time, the helper ratcheted up the clatter of the tambourine by several decibels, which made the whole spectacle even more unnerving.

I ran out into the bathroom. I could only see blurrily through my half-open left eye; the other was matted together with the blood from the rooster. "Go wash yourself," the bald man called after me, as if I really needed that instruction. I fumbled my way to the sink and turned on the hot water. I washed my face, rinsed the blood out of my eyes and took off my t-shirt, which was completely covered in red spatters. As I was scrubbing my naked chest with the washcloth, I noticed an unpleasant taste on my tongue, reminiscent of a mixture of zinc and molasses. I spat into the sink in disgust and furiously brushed my teeth. When I was finished, a hand reached around the crack of the door and passed me a loose-fitting cotton shirt, similar to the top garments my two visitors were wearing. I put it on and returned to the site of all the action. I found that everything had already been cleaned up. No trace remained of the rooster or any of the other accoutrements of the ritual. The dead bird had been consigned to the yellow suitcase along with all the other paraphernalia; with some effort, the helper carried it out into the hallway. The master gave me a businesslike handshake.

"All done. You will have no more problems with ifrit," he said, leaving me behind in the living room, reeling between fear, anger, and bafflement. For a moment I considered going after them, but then I realized that in my confused state I had no idea whether I should demand an explanation, berate them, or hurl abuse at them. Since my uninvited guests had left me in a state of utter emotional upheaval, I did nothing and instead lay down on my bed, still dressed, and fell asleep immediately.

When I woke up two hours later, I entered *ifrit* into the search bar on my smartphone. One of the hits took me to the website muslim-spirit.de. As it turned out, an *ifrit* was an "invisible vengeance spirit made of fire, with horns and the hooves of a donkey. This being can be extremely malevolent and inflict gruesome tortures on its human victims. It feeds on waste and excretes poisonous pellets. In order to rid oneself of this kind of creature, one must enlist the help of a Muslim exorcist, known as a *hodja*."

If I'm honest, I don't set much store by this sort of superstition. I believe in neither God nor the Devil—I only believe in the tangible, measurable world around us. Everything else is nonsense. That said, in the spirit of full disclosure I must add that after the visit from the two hodjas I never again had any problems with my apartment. My broken finger healed without any complications, and at some point I forgot the accident had ever even happened. I was not surprised that the unusual things that had happened did not repeat themselves. I never believed in a link between the visitors' appearance and the peace being restored in my apartment. I simply took it as a return to what I knew as the normal order of things.

✖

Some time later I saw a Sprinter van with a few pieces of wicker fur-niture inside it parked outside our front door. A young Ukrainian man was dragging boxes down the stairs. I knew immediately that Dany was moving out.

That same day, I ran into Rocket in the market hall on Marhei-nekeplatz. He emerged from the crowd of browsing shoppers just as I was biting into an overpriced grass-fed burger with a side of fries.

"Hello, my brother," he said, folding his hands together in the Indian greeting.

"Hi," I said.

"Are you not coming to yoga anymore?" he asked, without any accusation in his voice.

"I switched to kickboxing."

He looked at my plate.

"That looks good. Do you mind if I come sit with you for a moment, my friend?"

Although I didn't feel like talking to Rocket, I invited him with an encouraging gesture. I felt there was something he wanted to tell me. He seemed uncharacteristically tense, which, for all his studied Buddha-like equanimity, he wasn't quite able to conceal. Rocket sat down on the barstool next to me, called over the woman running the stall, and ordered a vegetarian burger with guacamole. I wolfed down a handful of fries and offered him some too. "Here you are, to tide you over."

He thanked me and gingerly took a few from the plate.

We were quiet for a moment.

"We didn't live up to our own expectations," he began abruptly. "I mean the generation that I'm a part of. We made mistakes."

He looked at me seriously and continued. "I'm aware of that—very much so, in fact, my brother."

"We all make mistakes," I said vaguely, since I didn't understand what he was getting at.

"That's true. You have to consider the situation we were in when I was young. It wasn't just that the Nazis were still alive—they held key positions in our country. Many older people were traumatized veterans, full of hatred and bitterness, and then poisoned by the National Socialist ideology on top of that."

Rocket mused for a moment. A film reel seemed to be playing in front of his eyes, shadowy figures flaring up in his mind.

"Everything we achieved was hard-won, accomplished in the teeth of opposition from these ignorant people. Gay rights. Women's rights. Refugee rights. You probably can't even imagine all that, since you're much younger than me. We had so little freedom. So we took it. We had to be selfish."

I didn't know what to say in response, so I just nodded, grabbed a toothpick, and started poking at bits of food between my teeth.

"We were frustrated, but they were also great times, my brother. The sixties were wild. Riots, ganja, parties all night long, and plenty of girls."

He gave me a conspiratorial wink. I didn't respond.

"Sometimes we took things a little too far," he added in a seemingly throwaway manner. Then his food arrived.

Rocket ate slowly, almost meditatively. I noticed his eyes were moist. At two o'clock I was meeting Max to try out the new centrifuge. I asked for the check. Before I left, I put a hand on Rocket's meaty shoulder. He was sitting on the bar stool strangely hunched and folded into himself.

"It's okay," I said gently.

KEY

STIEBEL HAD A RECURRING DREAM: a huge spider was sitting on the pillow in front of him. He'd cry out in fear and turn the light on. For a brief moment the creature would still be there, right in front of him, but then it would transform into creases in the rumpled bedsheets.

Once, while he was backpacking through Argentina, Stiebel had come down with a high fever. He woke up during the night and once again saw a huge spider right in front of his face. When he turned the light on, it was still there. This time the dream wasn't a dream at all—the apparition was real. Stiebel turned off the light and went back to sleep. The next morning the spider had disappeared—it had probably crawled off under the floorboards somewhere. That was when he'd understood that the terror he felt in his dream had nothing to do with real spiders.

✖

Stiebel hadn't wanted a housewarming party. He didn't really want anyone coming over—he was more of an introvert—but his boyfriend had insisted on it. "Oh, don't be a spoilsport, we should get to know our neighbors."

And so Stiebel had caved. He and Gerd had moved from Munich to Berlin just a month before and he realized the only way to make friends in their new home was to be sociable. After all, he didn't know a soul here except for his colleagues, and he hadn't really clicked with any of them.

The small gathering had barely begun, but already Stiebel regretted having invited these strangers into his apartment.

"So what do you do for work?"

A pudgy lady whom he guessed to be around sixty years old, her thick hair forced into a bun, had pressed herself upon him and was surveying him curiously through thick glasses.

"I'm a violinist."

"How interesting! Though I know nothing about classical music—I prefer listening to talk radio. Where do you play?"

"With the Deutsches Symphonie-Orchester."

"Don't you have that handsome Brit as your conductor?"

"No, that's the Philharmonic."

"Oh, that's right . . ."

For a moment the woman seemed at a loss, or maybe she was just pausing to catch her breath. But then, undaunted by his sour expression, she thrust out a hand speckled with liver spots.

"Belzig is my name, but call me Hertha. I live in the old coach house."

"Laurenz."

"How are you liking your new place?"

She moved in even closer to him; her eyes lit up with curiosity. Stiebel tried to discreetly back away, but the kitchen wall was right behind him. He threw a helpless look over at Gerd, who was busy talking to a wan, thin man whom Stiebel had heard introducing himself as Dr. Weissmüller.

"It's fine."

"It's a very old building, it has its quirks, you'll see," Frau Belzig said.

"Really? Everything seems fine to me," Stiebel replied dismissively. "Okay, the faucet in the bathroom is leaking, but I can live with that . . ."

Frau Belzig widened her eyes as if Stiebel had confided some-thing extraordinary.

"Well, something needs to be *done* about that. You're a sensitive man, an artist, you can't have a leaky faucet getting in your way."

"It's not getting in my way, it's just dripping, that's all," he said gruffly. Stiebel attempted to make his escape, but she was having none of it.

"You have to talk to Wondrak, the super," she said, wagging her index finger reproachfully. "He'll sort it out for you in no time." She scribbled Wondrak's phone number onto a piece of paper and pressed it into Stiebel's hand.

"If you'll excuse me . . ." Stiebel at last managed to disentangle himself and headed off in the direction of the drinks table.

✖

Frau Belzig had been right about Stiebel: he was sensitive; he needed his peace and quiet. The constant dripping *did* begin to get on his nerves. Soon after the day of the party, he opened up his laptop and looked up the customer-service hotline of the property-management company. He dialed and sat through a dozen renditions of "Für Elise." When no one answered the thirteenth time, he gave up and searched his pockets for Hertha Belzig's note, only to discover that he'd thrown it out.

As it happened, he ran into her on the street. After patiently enduring several minutes of chit-chat and gossip, Stiebel mentioned the faucet.

"The property management are hopeless, I could have told you that right away," she said. "Wondrak's your man."

"I lost his contact information."

"Oh, he's up there." Frau Belzig pointed up at a narrow window looking out onto the courtyard. "Why don't you stop by now? You just need to be aware—he's a bit . . . eccentric."

With that she launched into the details of the super's life and exploits. It turned out that Willy Wondrak was almost a hundred years old. No one knew his exact age, and none of the tenants had ever dared ask. He could still remember the famine at the end of World War One, the emperor's exile, and the turmoil of the Weimar years. As Wondrak hobbled around the courtyard, he would recount stories about those days in his gruff way, barely pausing for breath.

The most striking thing about Wondrak, according to Frau Belzig, was his voice. All that remained of it was a strained croak. This was due to a wartime injury: "The Russians shot him in the neck. It went clean through," she told Stiebel.

Sometime in the seventies, cycling home drunk, Wondrak had crashed his bike into the subway entrance at Wittenbergplatz. His left leg had been stiff ever since.

But despite the traces that a century of living had left on his body, Wondrak seemed agile and full of energy. Hertha Belzig couldn't explain where he found his strength. He'd been the super of 42A to 42E for fifty years and he had no intention of ever retiring from the job. He fixed whatever needed fixing, clambering up dizzyingly high ladders, cutting copper pipes to size, kneeling to pound loose cobblestones back into place. He insisted on strict order, though he constantly broke the house rules himself and only grudgingly complied with the law. "I'm too old to change," he'd rasp whenever one of the tenants complained about his brusque manner.

After the luxury refurbishment in 2009, Wondrak's position had been scrapped. The complex had been taken over by Trondheim Invest, a Norwegian real-estate company. However, the older tenants that remained—those who hadn't yet been bullied out of their homes by the new landlords—were suspicious of this impersonal service. "I always ask Wondrak for everything, bless his soul. And he'll never take any money," Frau Belzig ended her story.

✖

Stiebel walked up the stairs, rang Wondrak's doorbell, and waited. Nothing happened. He rang again. Suddenly, he heard a rustle from deep inside the apartment, as if an animal had been roused from its slumber. A shadow appeared in the spyhole. Then there was the sound of a key rattling and a chain being pulled back. Wondrak opened the door and eyed him suspiciously.

"Herr Wondrak, my name is Stiebel, we just moved into the front building."

"So you're the gentleman with the violin."

"Yes, I play with the Deutsches Symphonie-Orchester."

"I'm pleased to note you're observing the designated quiet hours. You play very well."

Stiebel felt relieved, although he couldn't quite put his finger on why.

"Frau Belzig thought you might be able to help me with a small problem. We've got a leaky faucet in the bathroom and I'm not very handy myself . . ."

Without another word, Wondrak buttoned up his cardigan and disappeared back into the apartment. Stiebel looked past him into the hallway, which had stacks of newspapers towering up on both sides, illuminated by a single low-energy lightbulb.

After a few minutes Wondrak returned. He had put on an army parka and was carrying a gray toolbox. Without speaking, the two men descended the stairs, crossed the courtyard, and went into the pale-yellow front building. Stiebel opened his door with the elaborate security key and led Wondrak through into the bathroom. Wondrak took out a rusty wrench and went to work on the faucet. "It's criminal how badly these things are made nowadays," he said in his rasping voice. Stiebel stood in the doorway. He felt unsure of himself in the old man's presence. Wondrak wiped his hands on a tea towel and narrowed his eyes at him.

"Don't you do any of this stuff yourself?"

"No, I'm hopeless at DIY."

"Well, you have to have the knack."

With a magician's flourish, Wondrak pulled a washer out of his toolbox. "They come in packs of five. I went right ahead and bought thirty of them."

He muttered something that sounded like a curse, though it was unclear who it was directed at: violinists with no talent for home improvement, the new property-management company, incompetent faucet manufacturers, or mankind as a whole.

With a few practiced twists of the wrench, Wondrak replaced the washer and screwed the faucet back into place. Then he threw the wrench back into the toolbox with a loud *clank!*

"Can I offer you a coffee?" Stiebel asked, helplessly.

"No thanks. Narrows the blood vessels. That stuff is poison."

"I'd like to give you some money for the repair."

"No thank you."

"Are you sure?"

"Positive."

"Is there anything else I can offer you?"

"No, nothing really. There is one thing though—let me give you a piece of advice."

"Of course. Let's go into the living room and sit down," Stiebel said, confused.

He took the old man over to the modern corner sofa by the grand piano, but Wondrak preferred to remain standing. He pointed at the large window that looked out onto the courtyard. "You know the lawn next to the remnants of that old shed—to the left of the parking lot?" he said.

"Yeah?"

"The owners want to put a playground there. A ridiculous idea! There are no small children here."

"Then why are they doing it?"

"Probably some stipulation from the planning office that they forgot about when they carried out the renovations."

Wondrak grabbed Stiebel by the shoulder. "Look, you own your place. Why don't you team up with some of the other residents and put a stop to this nonsense?"

"Well, to be honest, I wouldn't really have a problem with them putting a playground in over there."

The old super looked up at him, bristling with anger.

"Don't you see—we'll have youths loitering there and shooting up drugs!"

With these words, Wondrak turned on his heel and disappeared.

Stiebel told Gerd about the encounter, but they soon forgot all about it. The homeowners' meeting came around in early October, but no one raised any objections to the construction plans. Frau Spahn, who lived in the east wing of the building, showed up at the meeting eight months pregnant. She was delighted that the complex would be getting a playground.

Not long after that, a small digger rolled up to excavate a rectangular trench next to the skeleton of the old shed. On the second day the work had to be halted because the machine's engine broke down. Then a heavy frost set in and turned the ground rock solid.

✖

When Stiebel drove to rehearsals in the mornings, he threw on a thick puffer coat. On his way to Potsdamer Platz he barely noticed the world around him. The preparations for the performance of Stockhausen's *Helicopter String Quartet* were in full swing. The orchestra planned to use this mighty spectacle as a way to get out from under the shadow of their competitors, the Philharmonic.

The piece was to be performed as it was originally intended, with four helicopters. An air display team made up of Eurocopter Tigers had been specially requested from the Air Force. They would circle over Potsdamer Platz with a musician sitting in each helicopter. A livestream would be fed through into the concert hall, and there would be a simultaneous radio broadcast for the people listening at home. Stiebel had been designated first violinist and had a place in the helicopter at the head of the small squadron. The piece was demanding musically—it was fast; Stockhausen had sought to create a counterpoint between the rotor blades and the increasingly frantic strings, which were to buzz like a swarm of agitated wasps. All this was supposed to be accompanied by occasional full-throated cries from the players, a level of extroversion that Stiebel abhorred. The stress on his shoulders was considerable, but he went about his preparations in a calm, focused manner. Usually Gerd, who was doing a part-time training course to become a shiatsu therapist, would pick him up from work in their Audi.

On the weekends, they would drive to Potsdam and stroll around the old palace gardens to relax, and then visit the Posthof for a pub meal of calf's liver with apples and onions—a classic Berlin dish. On Sundays they occasionally went to the Volksbühne, the city's most iconic theater, to see one of its experimental productions.

On one of these nights—the second Sunday in November—damp snow was beginning to fall when the couple came out of the theater. Gerd held his coat over Stiebel's head to keep him dry as they got into the car.

Fifteen minutes later they parked in the courtyard of the building complex. A dense flurry was coming down now, and an icy wind was blowing in from the west. Stiebel pulled a small umbrella out of the glove compartment and got out of the car. But as he was opening the umbrella, a sudden gust of wind tore it from his grasp, hurling it high up into the air. He hurried after it, in the direction of the ruins of the old shed. The snow was falling so thickly that he could scarcely identify the outline of the shed's caved-in walls. Squinting, he tried to make out his umbrella in the shadows. He kept mopping away snowflakes from his face. Squalls of wind surged in rapid succession across the parking lot. Suddenly, over the din, he heard Gerd call out. He swung around, but saw only darkness. A cracked tile crunched under the leather soles of his shoes.

All at once Stiebel was reminded of the blue eyes of the wolf from the fairy tales of his childhood. He suddenly felt sure that he was being watched from the windows of the ruined outbuilding. He tried to swallow down the fear that surged up in him.

He peered into the winding labyrinth of the ruins. White light pushed through the cracks in the old brickwork, even though the moon was hidden behind a mass of clouds. Stiebel heard soft footsteps, like those of a child, in the snow. When he looked around, something grabbed him by the wrist and tugged at him, trying to drag him deeper and deeper into the maze of ruins. Snow-covered branches were poking through a crack in the wall—or were they fingers reaching for him? Stiebel tore himself loose and made a run for it, bolting out of the derelict shed. The steps behind him quickened. He flung himself forward into the darkness and fell. Fine clouds of powdery snow rose up all around him. As he lay there, trembling and helpless, a sharp pain burning in his ankle, his pursuer drew even nearer to him. The bowed figure was dressed from head to toe in black.

Stiebel looked up, horrified, but it was his Gerd's face he saw looking back down at him. His boyfriend helped him get up out of the excavated trench, brushing the snow off his coat. Stiebel was shaking. Gerd watched him, concerned, as he stopped and leaned against the driver's cabin of the digger to catch his breath. Then, when he seemed to have recovered somewhat, he linked his arm through his boyfriend's and they walked back to the house together in silence, the snow whirling around them. Whatever it was that Stiebel had sensed in the ruins—it was gone now.

It wasn't until he had warmed up by the radiator in the kitchen and Gerd had made him a cup of tea that Stiebel ventured to speak. He said that this concert, the intense pressure, must be playing on his nerves. "Promise me you'll take some time off when it's over," Gerd insisted.

"I promise."

✖

November passed, and Stiebel tried to put the episode out of his mind, but he didn't entirely succeed.

Early December brought a period of thaw, and the work on the playground started up again. The digger had been fixed by now. When Stiebel drove to work in the mornings, he greeted the workers who were ploughing up the ground and bringing in the metal rods for a swing set.

On December 6, St. Nicholas Day, he left the dress rehearsal in high spirits. He had played the piece extremely well, creating an electric flow with his fellow musicians. Afterward, the conductor had complimented him on his performance: "If you're only half as good at the concert as you were today, this will be a huge success." It had been the last run-through, but Stiebel felt confident and primed for the event.

When he got home, he threw his coat over a chair and strolled into the living room. Gerd was on a Skype call with his mother in Garmisch. They were talking about his shiatsu exam which was coming up in February.

Seeing Stiebel, Gerd gave his mother a wave goodbye and ended the call.

"So how did it go?" he asked.

"Perfect. Couldn't have gone better."

"That calls for a toast, don't you think?"

Stiebel's partner went and got a bottle of Spumante from the fridge and filled two champagne glasses. They sat down on the sofa. Gerd wrapped a strong arm around him. Stiebel felt his warm skin against his neck.

"How was your day?"

"Pretty uneventful. There was some commotion outside though."

"Where?"

"Downstairs, in the courtyard. The police were here. Not by our building—over there." Gerd gestured toward the construction site.

"What did they want?"

"I only know from hearsay, but Frau Belzig said that during the digging the construction workers found bones."

"What kind of bones?"

"*Human* bones. During the war, they used to assemble airplane seats in that shed. The year before the war ended, it was hit by a bomb. Apparently there are half a dozen people buried down there."

Stiebel groped for the back of the sofa.

"I know, it's not a pretty story. Maybe I shouldn't have told you."

Gerd's arm slid off his collar. He got up. Stiebel looked at him, but he couldn't read his partner's facial expression. Gerd folded a paper napkin and cleared the two glasses.

✖

The days were short now. It was still dark outside when Stiebel left the house on the day of the concert, the kitchen garbage dangling from one hand. As he was making his way over to the trash cans in the courtyard, he saw a light flickering in the distance. He opened the large container, and the smell of rot hit him. Stiebel felt sud-

denly sick. He threw in the bag and walked over to the parking lot.
He pressed his key fob. The taillights flashed on and off. Just before
he got into the car, he glanced back over his shoulder. Wondrak was
standing there, by the small construction site, stock-still, a tealight
cupped in his hands. Behind him the red-and-white tape that had
been used to cordon off the trench was flapping in the wind. Wondrak was staring straight ahead, into the darkness.

Stiebel made as if to greet him, but thought better of it.

When he got back later that afternoon, Wondrak was still standing there.

On the stairs Stiebel ran into Frau Belzig, who was just coming
back from the store.

"Can I give you a hand?"

"Thanks, that's very kind of you."

Stiebel took the large shopping bag from her.

"Say, did you notice Herr Wondrak standing out there all by
himself?"

"Yes, I did."

"He seems to be waiting for something."

"I think he is afraid that those dead people will have their peace
disturbed. Surely you heard about . . ."

"Yes, my partner told me."

"There's a group of youths who keep loitering around over there.
They even vandalized the digger last month."

"Seriously? How do you know?"

"The workers told me. They arrived in the morning to find the
carburetor broken, and some other parts too. Jimmied open and
smashed to bits."

Frau Belzig fished around in her coat pocket for the key to her
apartment.

"You're always on edge with these kids nowadays," she sighed.

Stiebel set her shopping down beside her.

"Funny—I've never actually seen any kids around here, have you?"

"Come to think of it, I haven't. Wondrak's the only other person I've ever seen around that machine."

With this, Frau Belzig thanked him kindly for his help, and they parted ways.

✖

That evening, eight hundred spectators had poured into the large concert hall, and a thousand curious onlookers had crowded onto Potsdamer Platz, where the concert was being shown on a huge screen. Stiebel put on his tails—Gerd had to help him with his bow tie—and did some warming up. An officer from the Air Force picked him up in a limousine and took him to the airport, where his three colleagues were already waiting for him. They climbed into their respective helicopters and flew the short distance to Potsdamer Platz. Stiebel barely noticed the crowds beneath him; he was looking intently at a monitor, watching out for his cues from the conductor. Stiebel played with full concentration, building up to the last crescendo with a mixture of passion and precision. When the applause erupted, he carefully leaned the violin against the chair and wiped his forehead with a handkerchief.

Later that night, Stiebel lay awake thinking about the concert. He was so hyped up he couldn't sleep. Counting sheep didn't work, and neither did the shiatsu relaxation techniques that Gerd had taught him. In the end, he tried to think about something completely different.

He recalled an article he had read about Emperor Rudolph II. His army had a regiment of dwarves and a regiment of giants. First the giants would attack, clubbing everything in their path to pieces. Their size and stature, however, made them an easy target for the archers. The losses among the giants were enormous. Then the dwarves would follow in their wake. They would clamber over the bodies of their dead adversaries and those of the giants that had been felled by arrows, and plunge their swords into their enemies' legs. This part of the attack was highly successful. The dwarves weren't particularly strong and the wounds that they inflicted on the soldiers were rarely fatal. But any military strategist worth their salt knows that an injured foe is worth much more than a dead one. A dead enemy is buried and gone in twenty minutes. An injured one saps the opposition's strength for months: field hospitals are required to treat him, a whole supply chain has to be mobilized to nurse him. While military doctors, nurses, cooks, and delivery boys are all preoccupied with his well-being, he himself is useless, unable to contribute to the battle. That's why the regiment of dwarves was more effective on the battlefield than the giants. But at the victory parades, the people only ever cheered for the giants. They laughed at the dwarves.

At 5:00 a.m. the next morning, the garbage men found Wondrak's corpse in the construction trench. It was frozen stiff, the left hand still clawed around the burned-out tealight. His military parka was unzipped. Other than that, there was nothing remarkable about Wondrak's body—it looked quite ordinary. Several hours later, a hearse pulled up and took him away. For the undertakers the incident was just one among many. People froze to death every winter in Berlin. Usually they were homeless; Wondrak's case was assumed to have been an accident, the result of dementia creeping up in his old age.

Stiebel found out about the super's passing from a notice that had been put up in the building. Someone had added the time and place of the funeral in pencil. He made a mental note of the date—it was the following Tuesday.

✖

When the day arrived, he took the morning off. He didn't tell anyone about his plans, not even Gerd. His GPS took him to the crematorium in twenty minutes—a new building that had won a host of awards. When he entered the lobby—its decor a neutral white—he found only two other mourners there.

Frau Belzig, a black shawl around her shoulders, waved and beckoned him over. She introduced him to Dr. Weissmüller, the former manager of the city library whom she'd brought along to the housewarming party some weeks before.

An officiant called the three of them into the chapel. Inside, Wondrak's casket had been put on display. It looked surprisingly small. There were no flowers or wreaths anywhere to be seen. The officiant motioned for the three of them to sit down on a bench before discreetly vanishing through a side door. Classical music sounded from a speaker—first Liszt, then Mahler. After a brief pause, the coffin, which was resting on metal rollers, slid discreetly through a hatch and out of sight.

Stiebel waited for a moment. When he saw the two other mourners get up, he followed suit and headed for the exit.

Dr. Weissmüller and Frau Belzig were waiting for him in the covered gallery just outside the building.

"Did you know him?" Dr. Weissmüller asked.

"Barely. As you know, we only moved in last August," Stiebel said. "How about you?"

"Oh, I've known him since the eighties. He was a real character. No one knew our neighborhood better than he did."

"Dr. Weissmüller is working on an interesting project at the moment," Frau Belzig said.

"I'm an historian by trade, and for the past few years I've been studying the history of the neighborhood. I always meant to ask Herr Wondrak about your building."

"Why?"

"Because of the POWs."

"Ten Polish prisoners of war," Frau Belzig explained. "The Nazis made them assemble seats for Junkers aircraft in that shed."

Dr. Weissmüller looked at Stiebel's questioning face.

"There was a wooden barracks next to the factory. Someone who lived around the corner in those days told me about it. The workers were locked in there every evening after their shift."

"Dr. Weissmüller had to tell the police all about it when the bones were found," Frau Belzig added, with a self-important look on her face.

"During an air raid in 1944, the factory was hit by a bomb in the middle of the night. It caused such a powerful explosion that the whole building came down. The barracks was buried underneath one of the exterior walls. The workers locked inside never stood a chance."

"Was Herr Wondrak already living in the building at the time?" Stiebel asked.

"He was the *Blockwart* in those days—one of those people put there to report back on the goings-on in the neighborhood to the Nazis. At least that's what the Residents Registry for 1938 says. I really wish I'd had the chance to ask him about it, but unfortunately it's too late for that now . . ."

"I'm sure he did nothing wrong," Frau Belzig said. "He was such a lovely man."

"Innocent until proven guilty. Let's just leave it at that," said Dr. Weissmüller.

At that moment, one of the crematorium staff appeared with a large plastic bag in her hand.

"Are you the next of kin? The undertakers gave us his coat."

Stiebel held out his hand. "I'll drop it into the donation bin."

✖

Stiebel drove Dr. Weissmüller and Frau Belzig home; they had both come on public transit. Then he turned his Audi into a side street and parked. He put a warm hat on before getting out of the car. Ice-cold sleet was coming down from gray clouds as he crossed the street. When he got to the Red Cross bin, he pulled Wondrak's parka out of the bag, then stopped, feeling a small object in the left pocket. He reached inside and pulled out an old key, its teeth rusty. He looked at the iron object, uncomprehending.

Five minutes later, Stiebel was standing over the construction pit beside the ruins. For a moment he hesitated. Then he threw in the key.

EX PATRIA

ON THEIR FIRST DATE AT Strothmann's, Tiger told Kelly about the novel he was working on. It was a sci-fi novel set in the year 2050, in a time when females had found a way to reproduce without men, who were now nothing more than superfluous sex objects. When they got tired of their lovers, they would put them on surfboards made of asbestos and force them to ride the lava stream that spewed out from Mount Etna. Some would manage to keep their balance for a moment before toppling into the viscous mass of molten rock. Perched on the crater's edge, the women would cheer at the men's excruciating demise.

Tiger spoke about its premise in great detail. But while it sounded intriguing to Kelly, Tiger had not asked much about her. In fact, it seemed at times as if he were talking to himself.

"I'm almost done," he said, taking a sip from his Strothmann's Special, a pisco sour with cinnamon.

"With what?"

"With the book!"

"Oh."

"It's still very rough at this stage. But my agent likes it."

That caught Kelly's attention. She didn't know anyone who had an agent.

"Wow, seriously?"

"Yeah, and my agent says—"

Before Tiger could launch into another anecdote, the waiter arrived with a bowl of peanuts. Kelly saw her chance to get her turn in the conversation.

"Well, I'm here to work on a film—that's why I'm supposed to be here, at least," she said hastily.

She told him that she had gone to Tisch and had shot her thesis project in the New York subway. "It was a short about the Elephant Man, whose story I transposed into the present day. I wanted to see how passersby would respond to the lead actor once the makeup artists had deformed his face with silicone prosthetics. We used hidden cameras, zooming in on the faces of the people rushing by on the subway platforms as they paused to gawk at him. After three months we had nine thousand views on YouTube."

"People who've been through a lot tell the best stories," Tiger said gravely, staring at an imaginary horizon.

Kelly looked at Tiger in awe. He was so different from the students at Tisch, who'd tried feverishly to act like artists but who, in the end, had just been wannabes.

Kelly and Tiger's romance began after he'd become her roommate. She was living in a converted convenience store on Harzer Strasse that had been turned into a short-term rental. The side facing the street had originally been the storefront—a light-bathed room that the owner had furnished with tastefully chosen Ikea furniture. Hanging on the wall was something you'd normally only see in the offices of ad agencies and media start-ups—a pair of deer antlers. Seeing her eyeing them, Ingo, who owned the property, had explained, "They're what you call *eight-pointers*."

Ingo was a fashion photographer and had bought the store on Harzer Strasse for a song in the late nineties. Ever since the hype surrounding Berlin had begun, he'd had back-to-back bookings. Almost all of the renters were people from the East Coast of the United States.

He and Kelly had quickly reached an agreement on the rent. It was more than the budget her parents had set her, but Ingo had agreed to her finding a roommate for the duration of her stay, so she'd posted a short ad online offering the second bedroom as a sublet.

That same day an anorexic cellist from Finland had showed up to look at the place. The young woman had looked at Kelly out of red eyes and talked emphatically about Stockhausen. The next person to stop by had been a Greek guy who was looking to brush up on his German. His name was Dimitri; he had a small paunch and a mop of curly hair. He was nice enough, but he was almost forty and she thought that was a bit too old for a roommate.

The third candidate was a young man: muscular, freckled face, plaid shirt. He was sucking on a lozenge because the air on the plane, he explained, had been very dry. He introduced himself as Tiger. He had just arrived from Budapest, where he had been giving a reading from his short-story collection. Tiger didn't feel like talking; Kelly's questions were met with silence. At the same time she found herself mesmerized by his cocky charm.

Tiger leaned back in one of the theater chairs that Ingo had managed to salvage when the Delphi theater had been redecorated. He looked around.

"Looks alright," he mumbled.

For a moment Kelly wasn't sure who or what he was referring to, whether he liked the apartment or was trying to pay her a compliment.

"There's a nice café around the corner. And we have an espresso machine."

There was silence for a moment.

"Shall I show you the room?"

"Sure."

They got up. Tiger had to press his way past her. His upper arm brushed her shoulder—it was big and firm, the result of many hours spent at the gym. She noticed the scent of his body, an almost unnoticeable mixture of salty tang and sandalwood deodorant.

The second bedroom had a double-glazed window with an old brass handle. If you went and stood next to the night-storage heater, you could look down into the courtyard. Below, there was a chestnut tree afflicted by parasites, whose sickly, speckled leaves blocked out the sun during the summer months. Next to the tree there was a glass container with a sticker on it instructing residents to refrain from throwing bottles in after 8:00 p.m. The room itself had wood-chip wallpaper, two Billy bookcases full of Ingo's photo albums, and a folded-out sofa bed covered with wine-red sheets. Next to it there was a bedside table with a designer alarm clock that responded to hand motions, along with a copy of Leni Riefenstahl's book of photographs of the Nuba tribe. Tiger flipped it open to a page showing a tribal warrior who had driven an ocher peg through his nasal septum.

"Wild piercing," he said, and shut the book. "So, how much?"

"What do you mean?" Kelly asked, flustered.

"For the room, what else?"

Kelly felt her face going pink. "Four hundred euros, including internet and electricity."

"I can do that. And what's the total rent for the entire apartment?"

"I'm paying eleven hundred euros right now, why?"

Tiger gave her an interested look.

"That's a lot of cash."

Money had never been an issue for Kelly—she had wealthy parents. Her father was on the board of Atlantic Cross, a large insurance company. Having money available on tap was a reassuring feeling. But at the same time Kelly felt that her world was too sheltered. She wanted to stand out—to be an artist who would create great things. If she was going to have to rough it to get there, then so be it. So she'd told her parents to put her on *minimum support*, which meant two thousand dollars a month.

"I'd pay three times as much for a place like this in New York," she said offhandedly.

Tiger seemed to like that answer. He fixed her with a smile that gave Kelly a deep, warm feeling inside.

She had planned to leave herself a cooling-off period before deciding who to offer the room to—after all, you should sleep on these kinds of decisions, at least for a night. Instead she accepted Tiger there and then. He moved into Harzer Strasse the next day with a backpack and two Samsonite suitcases.

Kelly hadn't expected their get-to-know-you drinks at Strothmann's would turn into a date. Still, she had enjoyed the evening, especially once Tiger stopped talking about his novel and started paying more attention to her. It was past midnight when they left Strothmann's and headed out arm in arm into Kreuzberg, following the canal. At some point they sat down on the grass peering out at the dark water. Tiger leaned over and kissed Kelly on the lips. He tried to press his tongue into her mouth, but she recoiled, taken aback.

"Sorry, does the cinnamon taste bother you?"

"No—you're moving too fast for me."

"But we'll kiss later anyway. Why pretend—why don't we just cut to the chase?"

Kelly thought for a moment before putting her hand on his. Her lips rounded into a *no*. He had to wait—she needed that much restraint from him, even if she *was* living in hedonistic Berlin.

"Let's go home first and get comfortable."

Tiger frowned, but let Kelly lead the way.

The next two weeks were an endless flood of images: Tiger with his laptop, sprawled in a Danish designer chair; Tiger writing (he wrote in longhand, scribbling in composition notebooks); Tiger sulking because he had writer's block; Tiger showing her his pictures from when he'd gone kite-surfing with his buddy Charles in Morocco; Tiger shaving in the bathroom, dressed in only a towel.

"You're in love," was Caro's diagnosis—Kelly's German friend whom she was in the process of filming a documentary about.

Caro was a performance artist, and was getting ready for an art piece in which she planned to cover herself with tar and hurl herself into a pile of goose feathers. She had found a supplier in Poland, but she couldn't be sure that the animals weren't being harmed in the process of obtaining the down. Although she had already told an acquaintance who worked for the culture pages of the *taz* newspaper all about the project, she was now toying with the idea of canceling the event.

"No way!" said Kelly, who was hoping that everything would go according to plan so she could finish her own film piece about performance art. She promised that she would help Caro find an alternative source for the feathers.

As Kelly's daily life in Berlin took shape, there were also some difficult moments with her new boyfriend. She didn't mind that Tiger had stopped paying his share of the rent, but sometimes he would suddenly become very moody. When he was like that, she'd try feverishly to read his every wish on his lips, even those he hadn't yet expressed.

"Do you know that you can be pretty uptight sometimes?" Tiger asked one night.

"Really?"

Kelly felt exposed.

"Don't worry. I have the perfect antidote." He grinned and pulled out a tightly sealed mason jar from his backpack.

"This is cha-cha, a Japanese algae."

The water plant was swimming in a murky broth. "Charles swears by it. It opens up the chakras."

Kelly's first instinct was to say no, but Tiger explained that cha-cha wasn't a drug. In Japan it was considered a natural remedy that brought body and spirit into harmony with each other. It was best shared with someone you loved—that way it sharpened your awareness for your partner. Kelly nodded her assent and forced a smile.

When Tiger fished the algae out of the jar in the candlelight, she felt the mixture of fear and exhilaration that tends to accompany initiations. Using his Opinel knife, Tiger cut the plant into two pieces of equal size. He put one in his mouth and handed Kelly the other. She took the algae and put it on her tongue. Before she could change her mind, the slimy tendril had slipped down her throat.

At first Kelly didn't feel any different—just a little drowsy. She got comfortable on the sofa. Tiger lay down next to her. He had taken off his t-shirt. They snuggled up to each other, tessellating like two spoons in a drawer. Tiger's hand wandered under her top. Kelly wanted to say something tender and romantic, but she couldn't seem to string the words together. Time passed; she didn't know how much. Then her eyelids fell shut. When she opened them again, she saw that the earth was a flat disk. The couch had changed into a rowboat. After rowing for what seemed like forever, she and Tiger reached the edge of the horizon. They saw the place where the oceans crashed into nothingness. As they were leaning over to look, the boat got pulled into the current. Tiger desperately tried to row against it, but his efforts were in vain—they drifted farther and farther from the coast. After a while Kelly could barely make out the shoreline anymore. When Tiger realized the dire situation they were in, he jumped into the water and paddled to a rock that was protruding from the ocean. Kelly called out for him to throw her a rope, but she wasn't sure if he had heard her. Tiger said something, but the roar of the water drowned out his voice. As Kelly was watching him, transfixed, the boat began to drift away from the rock. The current kept getting stronger and stronger. Kelly tried to fight it, but it was no use. She found herself gripped by a nameless fear. Just as she was about to cry out, she was hurled over the edge of the world and fell into the depth in an infinite spiraling descent.

Kelly screamed out loud, and all of a sudden she was back in her own life. She was stark naked. Tiger was asleep beside her on the living-room sofa; he too was no longer wearing any clothes. A strand of spittle dangled from the corner of his mouth. It was the middle of the night. Kelly felt lousy. She had a vile taste on her tongue. A window was open somewhere; she shivered. She got up and dragged the duvet from the bedroom and pulled it over herself and Tiger.

"And you're completely sure?" Tiger asked.

"One hundred percent. I got a test from the drugstore yesterday."

She handed him the stick. Three parallel blue lines were visible in the middle.

Kelly had suspected for some time that she was pregnant. She was surprised by how calm she felt about it now that she knew for sure. It was fate, she told herself, that had brought about this turn of events, not just a moment of addled judgment.

"And you want to have the baby?"

"Yes, absolutely."

She hadn't expected her boyfriend to be thrilled about the idea. But now she felt a coldness slide between them like a wall of ice.

Tiger laughed and slammed his hand down on the table.

"I hope it'll be a boy!"

He didn't sound enthusiastic.

"Aren't you happy?"

"I'm overwhelmed!"

He reached behind him and put on some music on his cell phone—a new song by 50 Cent. He got up and danced once around the kitchen table, his hair flopping over his eyes. Something wild had come over him; it scared Kelly.

That night they lay beside each other in silence—she with questions buzzing around in her head that no one could answer, and he dumbly brooding away beside her. At some point Tiger got up and walked to the fridge to get a glass of orange juice.

"There's blood here," his voice called out from the next room.

"What do you mean?"

"There's a blood stain in front of the fridge. Did you cut yourself?"

"Nope."

"Weird. Anyway, I'll clean it up."

The next few weeks went by as if nothing had happened. Tiger got up around ten and made himself a double macchiato using the espresso machine. Then he'd get a shower, take one of his composition notebooks, and head out to one of the coffee shops in the neighborhood, where he would write or lose himself in endless conversations with kindred spirits who validated his views on world events. Around noon Kelly would wake up. She took a long time to get going in the mornings, which had more to do with how much sleep she needed than with her being pregnant.

Kelly wanted to wrap up her film project about the Berlin performance-art scene as soon as possible. She'd planned a number of shoots, so she joined forces with Lucia, an Italian camerawoman. Lucia had a degree from the Film Academy, spoke five languages, and liked to wear clothes that showed off her curves. Her mother was from Naples, and she had inherited her jet-black hair and superstitious streak. There was a sister in Italy who had a drug problem, and Lucia had spent years sacrificing herself to take care of her. She wasn't on good terms with her parents because they had cut ties with their heroin-addicted daughter. "They couldn't handle the fact that she developed an addiction," she told Kelly. After a suicide attempt the doctors had committed her sister to rehab. Things didn't seem to be getting any better. When Lucia spoke of her sister in her deep voice, she seemed despondent. "She was born under a bad sign."

Meanwhile, Caro had started rehearsals. She had strewn her studio in Neukölln with packing peanuts to serve as a replacement for the feathers. Kelly and Lucia filmed the first of the run-throughs. At the end of the performance Caro recited a text that consisted of newspaper clippings that she'd collated together at random. Tiger seemed to be interested in the project: he wandered through the studio sucking on an e-cigarette. Sometimes he would just sit in a corner and watch Lucia as she screwed the camera onto her tripod and straightened it with a built-in level. In those moments she was completely absorbed in her work and her dark eyebrows would scrunch up. When she bent over to squint through the eyepiece, her whole body would go tense under her dress, like a predator about to pounce.

During the breaks from shooting Lucia and Tiger stood a little off to the side, talking in hushed voices so as not to disturb Caro's concentration. The subject matter of their conversations could not be inferred: as soon as Kelly got closer, they would break apart.

In the fifth week of her pregnancy, Kelly too saw the blood. Tiger had gone out for the evening with Charles. He had turned around at the door and told her that it was going to be a late night. They were planning on watching a boxing match that wouldn't be starting until the evening East Coast time—the middle of the night in Central Europe.

"I need my freedom," he said when she gave him a look. "I know," she replied.

When Kelly felt herself getting sleepy, she made a rooibos tea and stretched out on her bed in an oversized t-shirt. She picked up her book, an English-language edition of Wladimir Kaminer's collection of comic vignettes about nineties Berlin, *Russian Disco*. Three pages in she was asleep.

At some point, hours later, she sat bolt upright in bed. Her heart was pounding. Although she opened her eyes wide, she saw only blackness. She was convinced that she'd gone blind. Only after a moment of horror did she realize that it was dark and the middle of the night. She fumbled for the light switch and flipped on the lamp.

Now she was able to see, but the terror remained. Tiger still wasn't home. Something was buzzing outside, maybe a faulty streetlight. She felt as if she'd taken cha-cha again—the same feeling of despair was churning inside her. She reached reflexively for the glass of water on her bedside table, but it was empty. She made a deliberate effort to calm down by taking some deep breaths before rising to her feet.

Kelly went into the kitchen, turned the tap over the sink on, and drank directly from the cold stream of water. It was when she turned around to go back to the bedroom that she noticed the blood. There was a gleaming puddle next to the fridge. And she could see another red spot on the kilim rug: arterial blood, saturated with oxygen. From the fridge the trail led off toward the door, then on down the hallway toward the basement stairs, where a footprint from a man's shoe was clearly visible in the red smear. On the beige linoleum of the landing she saw the next stain. Had a burglar stabbed Tiger? The blood loss had to be considerable. The trail tracked along the banister all the way down to the spot where the people in the building left their strollers. There was a heavy door covered in graffiti that led on down into the basement. It was propped open. Kelly flipped the light switch and raced down the stairs.

If you imagined the basement of Harzer Strasse 53 as a living creature, the entrance was its throat. Steep steps led down from there—that was the gullet. The warren of aisles that ran between the wooden storage lockers were the guts. Down here in the basement's bowels it felt warmer than up by the door. The air was stale. Beer crates, chairs, broken televisions, and all kinds of furniture were piled up high all around her. Most of these things had been forgotten: a guitar that no one played anymore; an exercise bike that no one wanted to sit on; a playpen belonging to a child that had probably long reached adolescence.

Some things were covered by plastic tarps; only their outlines were visible. The basement was a strange organism: the objects fed to it were preserved even if they had long decomposed in the memories of their owners.

At the end of the aisle Kelly found another puddle. She paused for a moment, listening for a sound from anywhere in the basement's tangled innards. The timer switch for the lights tick-tick-ticked away; an electrical appliance was buzzing somewhere. She heard another noise mixed in with it, this one closer by—a wheezing sound, like a bellows sucking and blowing air in and out. Suddenly Kelly felt a lurch of fear—in this sprawling basement, in a strange house, in a strange country. She felt an urge to run out into the street. But she thought of Tiger and suppressed her flight instinct.

She walked past a pile of gray rubble. Now she had reached the farthest corner of the labyrinth. Drainpipes ran along the wall on either side. At the far end of the corridor, there was a circular opening in the wall with a stack of tiles piled up in front of it. It was as if the hole exerted some sort of powerful gravitational force—all the light seemed to be sucked inside it. Kelly froze again and stopped to listen. The wheezing sound was faster now, every quarter of a second. She approached the opening and peered into the darkness. Lying on the floor was a young man. He was naked and curled up on his left side. Perhaps he was asleep, but his chest was working hard, rising and falling rapidly. The truly bizarre thing, however, was this being's skin: it was milky white and translucent. Beneath his epidermis, Kelly could actually see his heart beating and the blood flowing through his veins. But somewhere in the finest capillaries there had to be a leak—a dark pool had formed next to the figure and was slowly getting bigger. The young man seemed peaceful, as if he didn't care. It was an image of ethereal beauty— like many things in this world that only exist in the moment and then just as quickly dissipate.

Kelly stretched out her hand to touch the sleeping figure. But at that moment the set time expired with a loud clack—the electricity cut out. The lightbulbs in the basement snapped off. Now

Kelly was seized by terror. In a panic she started to run. She hit her head on something, fell down, got back up. Rounding the next corner, she found she had reached a dead end. The basement had been confusing enough even with the lights on; now it seemed to be extending in all directions, a metastasizing monstrosity. Kelly was sure she wouldn't be able to find her way out of the maze. But she kept walking, as fast as she could. Only when she had reached the end of her tether and all that was left was despair, she suddenly saw a light. It was falling slantwise from a crack high up above her. The closer she got to the opening, the brighter it seemed to get— hope transmuted into waves of light. Kelly ran up the stairs, taking them two or three at a time, and burst out through the door into the brightly lit hallway. Just as she got back up to ground level Tiger came in through the front door. She threw her arms around him so forcefully that he almost lost his balance. She pressed her forehead against his collarbone. He smelled of alcohol and sweat.

In the emergency room at St. Joseph Hospital they took down her name and date of birth. They quickly established that her insurance (Atlantic Cross's international policy) would cover the costs of any treatment. After Tiger had led Kelly into the waiting room, he walked over to a vending machine and threw in two euro coins. Hot filter coffee streamed into the paper cup. He grabbed a handful of sugar packets and strolled back over to Kelly. She looked pale and was staring straight ahead of her. She was sitting next to a Turkish family who were fussing over their sixteen-year-old son; he had gotten his bike stuck in the tram tracks at Berlin Nordbahnhof train station on his way home from a party. Now he was cradling his right arm, which was broken above the elbow.

When the digital clock above the door changed to 3:00 a.m., a nurse asked Kelly to step into the examination room.

The doctor on call was named Dr. Ziegler. He had gelled-back blond hair and a cleanly shaven face that was reminiscent of silent movie stars from the 1920s. He sat down on a stool next to Kelly and began to ask her questions with calm professionalism. There was no cause for worry. Dr. Ziegler noted down: "Patient recounting incoherent stories. Hallucinations, cause unknown. Is a little worried on account of having taken a substance several weeks ago. Cause likely psychosomatic, somnambulism." He took his pad and wrote out a prescription for diazepam. He told her to take it easy for a while and led her to the door.

The next morning Tiger took Kelly down into the basement. He had insisted on it. At her urging they took a sharp kitchen knife down with them, just in case. But nothing threatening could be seen in the corridors, just towers of junk. One of the neighbors had collected furniture from the 1950s and at some point had lost interest in it. Since no one wanted to buy his kidney tables and orange upholstered armchairs, they were stacked up in his storage crate all the way to the ceiling. Right next to it was where Kelly had seen the hole. But there was no opening there—just a wheelbarrow leaned against the wall that belonged to the landlord. There was no blood to be seen anywhere either. "But you saw it yourself with your own eyes!" "Darling, I didn't see anything." "You *did*—by the fridge a few days ago." "That was from the lamb meat. There was a rip in the plastic bag."

Sitting around the apartment was making Kelly anxious. She felt like the walls were closing in on her. But there was no point dwelling on the events of the previous night. She was feeling better now, it was as if nothing had happened. The pills the doctor had prescribed were lying unopened in the drawer of her bedside table. A garbage truck came rumbling past outside. Kelly just needed to get out of the apartment, which despite its spaciousness seemed claustrophobic and was depressing her. Around 3:00 p.m. she set off on foot by herself to Caro's studio. She was supposed to meet her camerawoman there to look at the material from the last day of filming, but Lucia showed up an hour late. She was unusually monosyllabic; she didn't come out with an apology, nor did she want to talk about the footage she'd shot at the rehearsal. At one point Lucia did give her friend an appraising sideways look, but Kelly didn't notice it.

"I think I'm losing my mind," Kelly said abruptly.

She breathlessly recounted the events of the previous night, the blood stains and the apparition in the basement. Lucia listened attentively. "There are things that are outside the scope of our imagination," she said.

"So I wasn't just hallucinating because of that stupid algae?"

"Sometimes things happen to people that are so momentous that they continue to reverberate through to the next generations. Should we forget these events, those involved will remind us of the unredeemed guilt. That's what my mother told me."

Kelly wanted to know more, but Lucia responded evasively. She sank back into silence for the rest of the afternoon. She seemed agitated and distracted; when she was trying to back up one clip she ended up almost deleting it instead. Around five she suddenly gathered up her things. "I have an appointment," she mumbled and grabbed her puffer jacket.

Now Kelly was left there by herself. A coffee machine was gurgling in the room next door, which Caro had rented out to an architect. Someone said something about a meeting. At the far end of the courtyard mangy-looking pigeons were pecking at a crumpled-up pizza box from Pizza Pronto, an Austrian franchise.

In the stairwell of the building on Harzer Strasse, Kelly ran into Ingo, who had just bought a new charger for his cell phone at the Media Markt on Alexanderplatz. She asked him if he could come up to her apartment for a few minutes—there was something she needed to ask him. Ingo said sure. He was meeting his brother that night, who ran a wine store in Charlottenburg. He still had to take care of a few emails before then but that wouldn't take him very long.

Ingo followed Kelly into the living room and sat down on the sofa. He put the plastic bag with the charger down on the floor in front of him.

"What's up? Do you need help with the furnace?"

"No . . . It's about . . . feelings I had. It's hard to explain."

"Tell me in English."

Ingo made a few encouraging noises and put a hand on her shoulder.

She swallowed her embarrassment and told him what had happened. She described every last detail, from the night she and Tiger did cha-cha to the alabaster skin of the young man in the basement.

"I was dreaming with my eyes open. And now I'm wondering whether there was something *to* that dream."

She hesitated. Ingo coughed uncomfortably. "We've all had a bad trip at some point. Sometimes you can have a delayed reaction. I wouldn't touch that stuff anymore if I were you."

"Sorry," Kelly said, dejected. "It's just—you can't imagine how realistic it was."

"What you saw in the basement is probably because you've heard something about what went on down there. Sometimes people will talk about what happened back then—you know, the thing with the Wall."

"What thing?"

Ingo looked a little worried. "I thought you knew. I hope this isn't going to freak you out."

"No, please tell me."

"The building was just a few meters from the Berlin Wall. In the seventies some people tried to dig a tunnel underneath the death strip—the no man's land between the two Germanys—from here. They wanted to smuggle a woman across the border from the East. I don't know how it all ended, but there was a shooting. The entrance to the tunnel was on the east side of the basement. As far as I know, there's nothing left of it."

"That's a crazy coincidence—I didn't know anything about that."

"Yeah, pretty crazy," said Ingo without real conviction.

Kelly pressed him for more details, but he didn't have anything else to add to the story.

On his way out the door, Ingo mentioned that about a year before, a group of people had turned up who wanted to put a commemorative plaque on the building. Who they were and why the idea never came to fruition he didn't know, but maybe the property-management company still had their contact details. If she was interested, he could try to find out.

That afternoon, as Kelly was sitting in the Kebab King on Oranienstrasse with Tiger, she suggested that they move out of the apartment on Harzer Strasse. Tiger scoffed at the idea—he wouldn't hear of it. He made his "Tiger is annoyed" face, his eyebrows shooting up skyward. Kelly backed down immediately.

The sun broke through the clouds. Berlin seemed full of happy young people, most of them tourists.

By that same evening she was already regretting the fact that she hadn't been able to sell him on the idea of moving. Maybe she should have looked for a new apartment first, one that he'd have liked. A place with bigger windows and a comfy sofa for him to write on (he never worked at a desk out of principle: "Poison to creativity," he said). He would have been happier about Kelly's idea if she had, she was sure of it—he would have packed his Samsonite suitcases and followed her to Prenzlauer Berg or Friedrichshain. Instead she was lying in bed alone in the apartment on Harzer Strasse, trying in vain to focus on the book she was reading. Tiger had been in a huff all day. Around nine he went off to the Ankerklause bar by himself. Kelly dreaded his moods. But at the same time she knew she had to be patient with him—he needed room to breathe.

Kelly heard mattress springs squeaking somewhere on one of

the higher floors. Probably it was the caretaker having sex with his new girlfriend, a Georgian woman in her forties who seemed to be chronically anemic. The walls were very thin, but it wasn't the noise that was distracting Kelly. She'd really needed to pee for the past half hour, but she didn't want to go to the bathroom because she was afraid she would see blood again. She knew full well there was nothing there. But what good was her common sense when she was lonely? She grabbed her cell phone and called her parents. A familiar sound resonated: American dial tones. She let it ring twelve times, then she gave up. Her father was in the office; her mother was probably at the store. Kelly fished the packet of diazepam out of her drawer and unfolded the leaflet. On the back it said, "Not suitable for pregnant women." Had she told Dr. Ziegler that she was expecting a child? She couldn't remember. Instead of the full dose, she only took half a pill. She didn't have any water by her bed, so she gathered some spit in her mouth and swallowed it down with that.

The next morning, Tiger was lying next to her. She hadn't heard him come in. Kelly got up and walked over to the espresso machine. Since Tiger showed no signs of waking, she made herself a latte.

As she was going into the living room, someone rang the doorbell. It was Ingo.

"I had a chat with the woman from the property-management company. She remembers those guys with the commemorative plaque too. They were former Stasi officers—unpleasant types. She gave them the cold shoulder."

"Shame, I guess I won't be able to find anything more out then," Kelly said, disappointed.

"Well, actually . . . they left a phone number. I wrote it down for you."

Ingo flashed her an encouraging smile and handed her a folded piece of paper before saying goodbye.

When he had left, Kelly took out her cell phone and dialed the number that Ingo had written down.

A frail-sounding male voice answered.

"Are you calling about the reading?"

"Yes," Kelly lied.

"Tonight at 6:00 p.m. at the Starsky bookstore in the Lichtenberg megamall."

Before Kelly could thank him for the information, the person on the other end of the line had hung up.

She was supposed to go to a camera equipment rental at six to pick out a wide-angle lens with Lucia. She decided to move the appointment. But when she called her friend, Lucia let it go to voicemail, so Kelly sent her a brief text instead. Two minutes later she got a curt *OK*.

The megamall in Lichtenberg had been thrown up in the nineties just opposite the S-Bahn station. It was surrounded by grim prefab tower blocks from the communist years, which their new owners had tried to spruce up with a fresh coat of paint. But the turquoise patterns and yellow diamonds didn't make the buildings any more appealing; one error in aesthetic judgment had merely had another plastered over it. In these surroundings, the shopping mall seemed completely out of place, a multistory, glass-fronted behemoth that you could tell had been mortared with the cold sweat of investors. Although it sprang from a different political system than the tower blocks, it was no less soulless.

Walking in through the main entrance, Kelly was immediately besieged by elevator music. On the screens of the Victoria's Secret store, girls were prancing around who looked for all the world like underage prostitutes. A salesgirl with stick-on nails was listlessly arranging lacy acrylic panties from right to left. Next to the lingerie store there was a drugstore. An almost completely bald man was waiting at the checkout to pay for a caffeine-based hair-loss remedy. The corridor opened onto the main concourse of the megamall, where a glass elevator was gliding up to the top floor. All the way at the top there was an electronics store. Kelly doubted she'd be able to find a bookstore in this place. She went over to a fast-food restaurant and asked the man behind the counter. To her surprise he knew Starsky: third floor immediately on the right, next to the escalator.

When Kelly got there it was two minutes to six. Apart from the sales clerk—a resolute-looking woman with designer glasses— the store was empty. When Kelly asked her about the reading, the woman gestured at several rows of chairs in the back. She sat down on one of the folding chairs and waited. At exactly six a dozen people emerged from the crowds outside. Several of them had been drinking filter coffee from large paper cups at Coffee Nation. Others seemed to have cut straight through the shopping mall without partaking of its offerings. No one was under sixty; most were over eighty even— gray men and women in saggy pants and faux-leather sandals.

Moments later a wiry man with a gray crew cut and thick, high-diopter glasses sat down facing the crowd. The book he was presenting was titled *Main Department II of the Ministry for State Security*. He opened it somewhere in the middle and started reading in a flat monotone. Kelly struggled to make sense of the ceaseless string of names and numbers. Clearly the author was an expert on East Germany's secret police force—he'd probably even been a Stasi officer himself, just like most of his aged listeners, whose rigid military posture gave them away. The book was about the GDR's counterintelligence and its greatest achievements. But Kelly got the impression that the author was beating around the bush. Whenever it got exciting, the text became vague. It would refer to *sources*, *meetings*, and *operations* without ever saying what exactly they were. The audience did not seem to be bothered by this. Kelly looked around. Several of the listeners were nodding approvingly; others were just staring ahead with an expressionless look on their faces. Exactly one hour later the author said a few concluding words and brought the reading to a close. Chairs scraped the floor; two or three guests applauded briefly, and then the room emptied out as quickly as it had filled. Seconds later the elderly people could no longer be distinguished from the crowd of shoppers.

The author exchanged a few words with the store clerks, took his briefcase, and headed for the exit. For a moment Kelly debated whether to go after him and talk to him, but then she decided against it, feeling awkward. Instead she went to the checkout counter and leafed through his self-published book. A few of his other works were on display beside it. One of them was called *The Wall Casualties Among the East German Border Troops*. Kelly picked it up and flipped to the table of contents. Chapter 10 was called "Hero's Death on Harzer Strasse." Kelly snapped the small volume shut, her heart pounding, and fished a twenty-euro bill out of her wallet.

Once she got back home, she lay down in bed next to Tiger, the book in one hand and her laptop in the other, with translation software open. She skimmed the first few pages. They were about East German border guards who had died on duty, trying to "defend the Wall." She hurriedly flipped ahead to Chapter 10, which started with a description of how the Stasi were shadowing an individual called S., who had traveled into the GDR on a West German passport. It soon became apparent that this man—referred to variously as a "smuggler" and a "known trafficker"—had gotten in touch with a young bookbinder by the name of Gabriele Fuchs. S. wanted to help Gabriele "desert from the republic" so that she could be reunited with her lover, the West German citizen Bernd Abele. The border troop had been instructed to catch Gabriele and her helper in the attempt and destroy the escape tunnel. The arrest went spectacularly awry. S. and Abele drew their weapons. In the pursuit of the fugitives back through the tunnel, one border guard was fatally injured. "Lieutenant Stahnke was a hero," the chapter concluded. "His murderers escaped their just punishment." On the final page there was a photo of the young man that Kelly had seen lying lifeless in the basement. He was wearing a uniform and looking straight into the camera. His downy facial hair and large, close-set eyes gave him a childlike quality that he was trying to conceal with a decisive expression. He was all of nineteen years old—an age where death is just a rumor from stories told by older people. The caption read, "Lorenz Stahnke, victim of the Berlin Wall."

"That's him—that's the guy I saw downstairs!"

Tiger mumbled something inaudible. He was staring at the screen of his smartphone. Something had popped up on it that seemed to tickle him. The corners of his mouth had curled up into a smile. Kelly was annoyed. She looked over his shoulder to find out what it was that was so important. Tiger had a chat window open, but the moment his girlfriend looked over, he closed the app. "Darling, there's something I need to go take care of," he said and jumped up.

"Me too," she said, but Tiger had already disappeared into the hallway.

Kelly leaned back. She looked at her hand. It was trembling slightly. She went into the bathroom and took two diazepams.

The house was a ten-minute walk from Steglitz station. The facade was beige and could have done with a lick of paint. Underneath the doorbell there was a rectangular enamel nameplate with dark blue letters that said ABELE. The house had been bought by the current resident's father. Abele Senior had built a sausage-skin factory in Iran in the 1950s. He had exported the sheep gut to West Germany and sold it to the Südfleisch corporation, earning himself a small fortune. After the Khomeini revolution, his business operations had come to an abrupt end; the factory, complete with all the machinery, was seized and made the public property of the young Islamic Republic. Abele recalled his father's return and the stories of his adventurous escape over the mountains to Turkey. He showed Kelly a picture of the deceased patriarch. Father and son looked remarkably similar—they both had a round face, a bald patch and a mischievous facial expression. They had the confident ease of people who thrive in a capitalist economy.

Abele paused and poured Kelly some more jasmine tea. The china clinked softly. "But I'm sure you didn't come all the way here to talk about my father," he said.

She looked at him, but didn't reply. She had briefly talked to him on the telephone and told him why she was getting in touch. To her surprise he had invited her over straightaway. He had sounded relieved, like someone who needs to get something off his chest.

Abele took a careful sip of his tea. Then he started talking.

He spoke at length, musing on how unpredictable love was, reminiscing about the first time he'd seen Gaby, the secret rendezvous and passionate letters. It was a relationship that never should have been: Romeo and Juliet caught between the fronts of the Cold War.

"As the months went by, I became convinced that I needed to liberate my beloved from East Germany—a state that wouldn't allow her to leave, not even for a short visit in the West," said Abele, choosing his words carefully.

"Through a business associate I got in touch with the escape helper Richard S. who was a staunch anticommunist and wanted to inflict as much harm on the East German dictatorship as he could. It was his idea to dig a tunnel underneath the Wall. He obtained the tools and got in touch with the owner of the convenience store on Harzer Strasse from whose basement the operation was to be carried out."

"That's where I live," Kelly interjected.

"Yes, you mentioned that."

Abele cradled the teacup in his hand, reminiscing.

"I paid him ten thousand deutsche marks and we started digging. I worked like a man possessed; for weeks on end I barely saw daylight, just the dim cone cast by my headlamp. Since the tunnel was just thirty-five inches high, I had to shovel on my knees. By the end they were covered in scratches and scabs. In July we broke through to the surface next to a poplar tree, some two hundred meters east of the Wall. The mouth of the tunnel was obscured by the tree trunk."

"Was Gaby waiting for you there?"

"No. You see, we had no idea when we would be ready. So S. went to pick Gaby up from a meeting place they had agreed upon. But before he headed out, he pressed a loaded weapon into my hand—a small-caliber Smith & Wesson revolver. At first I declined. I was a conscientious objector—I'd never used a gun before. But S. insisted. He said the enterprise was very dangerous. Everyone knew the GDR's border troops were under orders to shoot fugitives. Finally I gave in and took the weapon."

"What happened then?"

"Around midnight that same evening, I crawled on my own through the tunnel to the East and positioned myself behind the tree to wait for Gaby. I had no idea that our adversaries had long gotten wind of the plan, and that a small tactical unit had taken up positions in the rental property directly across from me. When Gaby arrived, everything happened very quickly. S. called over to me 'They're onto us, we're fucked!' He seemed to be in a complete panic. Before I could react, he had disappeared into the tunnel. I pulled Gaby to me. She was trembling all over. I could hear footsteps and shouting coming out of the darkness. I showed Gaby the hole and crawled in ahead of her. She followed right behind me. About halfway through she called out to me that someone had grabbed hold of her thigh. She was crying hysterically. I heard loud noises that sounded like a scuffle. When I pointed my flashlight behind me, I saw, to my horror, that Gaby was being dragged away from me. I drew my gun and called out to her to duck. When she lowered her head, I saw a uniform jacket behind her."

"I had no idea the guy was so young. He'd ended up with the Border Troops more or less by accident. He'd been planning on going to college after his time in the service. He was a smart guy; he'd been nominated for a physics prize in high school."

Abele fell silent. Kelly nervously shifted in her seat. When her host had regained his composure, he finished the story. He'd been acquitted in West Germany; it was ruled self-defense. He broke up with Gaby a year later. "After that night nothing was the same. We continued to write each other letters for a while. She died in Kassel in 1996. It's odd that you want to know about all this. It's been decades since anyone's brought any of this up to me."

Just after Tiger had moved out of Kelly's apartment, she saw the blood for the last time. A loud knocking sound woke her up in the middle of the night. Someone was pounding frantically on the door. For a moment she thought Tiger had come back. But when she stumbled into the hallway and opened the door, there was no one there. On her way back to bed she saw a single red drop running down her thigh.

In the hospital Dr. Ziegler noted down: *Miscarriage, fourteenth week. Patient remains very weak. No signs of sepsis.*

DOUBLE-DECKER

THE BOUNDARY BETWEEN LIFE AND death isn't where we think it is. I now know that there are revenants among us—people who walk this Earth but who in reality are dead. I cannot provide an exact figure as to how many of these beings there are, but they exist. I saw one of them with my own eyes. Before, dear reader, you dismiss me as a crazy woman, I'd like to tell you who I am and how I arrived at this knowledge.

My name is Beatrice Aue. I'm forty years old, single, originally from the Rhineland. I actually come from nobility, though I dropped the *von* in my name. The title brought my father only bad luck—after the fall of the Berlin Wall he spent years attempting to reclaim our ancestral home in East Germany, ruining his finances and his health in the process. He died when I was seventeen years old. I'll spare you the details.

Suffice it to say that my father's death was a great shock for me, and sometimes I suspect that this is why nothing bothers me more than losing control over my life. This is likely why I am so structured in everything I do. I don't see my thoroughness as compulsive or constraining. I'm definitely up for adventure and excitement every now and again and, in sports especially, I like to push my limits. The only thing I don't like at all is air travel. I'm afraid of flying—perhaps because it involves giving over control to a faceless pilot and the vagaries of technology.

As for my finances, they're in pretty good shape. Until recently, I worked at a Berlin-based market-research firm where my liking for order and organization came in handy. The company had a very diverse portfolio of clients—from banks to sporting-goods manufacturers; from software developers to world-renowned pharmaceutical companies.

We researched the purchasing behavior of various demographics, or focus groups. We surveyed them by means of innocuous, informal conversations to keep their responses spontaneous, using methods from statistics, sociology, and psychology. I liked the job very much and I was very good at it. My superiors knew they could rely on me and admired my work ethic. With time, I caught the clients' attention as well.

About three weeks ago I got a call from Bernhard Laske, the head of marketing in Europe for an American-based tech company. I'd been in contact with him before, and knew him to be a pleasant and competent business partner. He broke the ice by making a throwaway joke that I don't recall now, and then segued into asking me to meet him. He wouldn't clarify why he wanted to see me, but stressed that I was not to tell anyone. Though I wasn't sure what all the mystery was about, I agreed to meet him on Wednesday evening in the lobby of a hotel on Gendarmenmarkt square.

The night of our meeting, I chose an outfit befitting the conspiratorial occasion: a dark blue merino wool dress, a small purse and flat shoes. As I stepped through the revolving doors into the hotel lobby, Laske came toward me down the marble spiral staircase that led to the mezzanine. He too was dressed discreetly, in a suit with a gray handkerchief poking neatly out of his breast pocket. On anyone else it would have looked old-fashioned, but it made him look mature and effortlessly sophisticated. We greeted each other with two quick kisses on the cheek. Then he took me to a small oyster bar in the back of the lobby. We sat in a booth at some distance from the other guests and ordered a dozen *fines de claires*. First we exchanged some chitchat about the current Anselm Kiefer exhibition that Laske had tickets to, although I got the impression he wasn't seriously interested in art. Then our conversation moved on to business matters. He didn't waste much time getting to the point: "My company would like to offer you an assignment. It's you personally that we want—not the institution you work for."

"I'm very satisfied with my job. I can't just walk away," I replied without skipping a beat.

"We know that. We're not talking about a permanent position here—I'm not trying to poach you. I'm hoping to get you on board for a temporary assignment that we feel only you can be trusted with. You are intelligent, diplomatic, and highly professional. It's a very delicate matter, quite a challenge—but one for which you would be generously compensated."

Like anyone, I enjoy getting compliments, and so I was more than happy to hear him out.

"If you are trying to pique my curiosity, you've succeeded."

Laske leaned back and gave me a winning smile.

"We'd like to book you on an exclusive basis for a ten-week period. If you say yes, I'll transfer a two-hundred-thousand-euro advance to you immediately. If you bring the assignment to a successful conclusion, you will get an additional bonus in the form of one hundred thousand euros."

I swallowed. While I made good money in my job, this was a completely different ball game. Laske surveyed my astonishment with some satisfaction, like a magician who has just pulled a rabbit out of his hat.

"And what do I have to do for that?" I asked.

"It's an assignment that involves a lot of finesse. Unfortunately, there's not a lot I can tell you about it. This request comes all the way from the top, from N— himself. He'll brief you personally."

Of course I knew N—. He was on the list of the world's richest people. His net worth was somewhere between 30 and 50 billion dollars—no one knew exactly. He'd built his company from the ground up in the eighties. By now it was a household name.

N— was something of a recluse. In all these years I'd seen at most two or three blurry paparazzi shots of him in the papers. His professional activities were as legendary as they were eccentric. I read somewhere that he wanted to mine raw materials on the moon; he'd invested in a company that was developing electronic invisibility cloaks; and he owned a laboratory in which people were working on creating a software copy of the human brain. He was also known for his unparalleled commitment to philanthropy. His foundation supported projects that gave children in developing nations access to a first-rate education. It was said to have an eight-figure budget at its disposal.

"This all sounds a bit too good to be true," I said skeptically. "There has to be a catch."

"There's no catch. And we're happy to give you the option of withdrawing from the assignment in the first three weeks. However, we would ask that you sign this in advance . . ."

Laske pulled a folded sheet of paper from the inside pocket of his suit jacket and slid it across the table. I scanned the document. It was a nondisclosure agreement that wasn't much different from the ones we had our market-research participants sign. The only thing that stood out was the unusually high penalty in the event of a violation—it was a five-figure sum.

"You guys are serious about not wanting me to talk," I said.

"We know we can trust you," he replied without blinking.

"So why the gag order? It's not about some scandal, is it? Did N— get himself into something?"

Laske cleared his throat disapprovingly.

"Nothing of the sort. You're going to have to trust me—that's all I can tell you right now."

"Do I have some time to think about it?"

"I'm afraid not."

I looked him straight in the eye. He didn't avoid my gaze.

"Okay, I guess I'll just have to see what's in the grab bag later," I said. I took a ballpoint pen from my purse and signed on the dotted line.

A faint smile played across Laske's lips. Clearly he'd read me right. I was unable to resist a modest frisson of excitement as long as I still had some sense of my bearings.

"So we've reached an agreement," he concluded with satisfaction.

"Looks that way."

I kept my cool and took a deep gulp from my champagne flute. We decided to order another half-dozen oysters. The rest of the evening Laske was unusually monosyllabic. I suspected he didn't want to inadvertently give anything away. When we said goodbye, he handed me an envelope.

"You will have to leave tomorrow evening to meet N—. I've already printed out your ticket. Oh, and by the way, have a look at your bank balance in the morning."

Once I was in the taxi, I opened the envelope. It contained a business-class plane ticket to Perth, Australia. There I had a connection to West Island which, as a search on my smartphone told me, was one of the Cocos Islands in the Indian Ocean. Population: six hundred; highest point of elevation: thirty feet above sea level. Climate: tropical. My heart was pounding, though whether it was from the exhilaration of taking on this job or from dreading the flight, I wasn't too sure.

The next morning, I woke up early. I stretched out in bed and fumbled for my glasses. Last night's meeting seemed like a dream. Without really expecting to see anything, I opened up my laptop and tapped in the passcode to my online banking portal. To my astonishment, I saw a payment of two hundred thousand euros had gone into my account. I couldn't believe it, but there it was, in black and white: two hundred thousand euros! I stared at the zeros behind the comma, dumbfounded. What was I supposed to do with all this money? Buy an apartment? Blow it? Donate it to help end world hunger?

After some time, I pulled myself together, called the office, and told them I had a family emergency and wouldn't be able to come into work for the next few weeks. My boss's assistant hesitated for a moment—she could probably tell from my voice that I was lying. Finally she wished me good luck and hung up.

I started packing. As I was picking out t-shirts, I began to steel myself for the journey. As I mentioned earlier, I'm afraid of flying. I wasn't too worried about the long-distance flight to Perth: I'm used to going on jumbo jets. But the connecting flight didn't inspire a lot of confidence. From the Australian mainland, a twin-engine Embraer would be taking me to West Island. I was sure that a small charter plane like that was not equipped for such a distance—more than twelve hundred miles. As I was googling the maximum ranges of different airplane types, I discovered by chance that the Federal Aviation Administration's statistics ranked West Island the fourth most dangerous airport in the world. The landing strip was situated on a narrow band of coastline and was really too short for jets. To make matters worse, wind shear occurred year-round—the pilots had to try to compensate for it with all kinds of heart-stopping maneuvers.

I logged into my online banking once again and trained my eyes on those five zeroes. I swallowed hard and resolved to be brave.

Twenty-three hours on a plane, four in-flight meals, and ten calming chamomile teas later, I was looking down onto the Indian Ocean from a comfortable two-story Qantas Airbus. I was still relaxed—I could still pull out at this point.

From thirty-five thousand feet up in the air, the ocean seemed peaceful—a large piece of shimmering blue cloth that covered the Southern Hemisphere, from Antarctica to Dar es Salaam. We were heading toward Australia from Singapore, where the sea meets the continent of Asia, with its billions of people. To the north, the Indian Ocean crashed onto the empty beaches of the Andaman and Nicobar Islands, whose tribes were still living in the Stone Age. This was an ocean of contradictions—ice-cold and warm, densely populated and desolate, shallow and more than five miles deep.

I hoped I wouldn't end up at the bottom of it.

When the landing flaps extended with a loud whirring noise, I felt the palms of my hands starting to get sweaty. I shuddered as I remembered that the worst still lay ahead of me.

The transfer in Perth went off without a hitch. Compared to the behemoth on which I'd come from Europe, the Embraer looked like a toy. As I tried to stuff my wheeled carry-on into the cramped overhead bin, my imagination began to run wild. Suddenly I was convinced a crash was inevitable. We would likely miss the island altogether because some instrument had been wrongly calibrated. We'd circle for hours until the kerosene ran out and the aircraft went into a barrel roll, followed by a terminal dive. I could picture the final moments vividly. We would spiral faster and faster, spinning down from the tropopause toward our own deaths. The nitrogen would boil out of my blood; my intestines would bloat like balloons; my lungs would collapse. Seconds later I would lose consciousness—by the grace of God, or faulty equipment, depending on how you looked at it.

Ten minutes later, after briefly taxiing, the jet shot up vertically into the azure sky. I broke out in a cold sweat. The man sitting next to me gave me a worried look out of the corner of his eye. At that moment, we hit some turbulence, and the plane lurched. After some time, I decided I couldn't bear any more agitation and closed my eyes.

Half an eternity later we made a sharp right turn and landed at a concrete airfield that had been built along a narrow beach. Three heavyset Malay women in colorful robes waved up at us through the whirlwind of sand. The pilot deactivated the thrust reverser and allowed the plane to taxi to a standstill. Workmen in faded t-shirts shoved an aluminum staircase up to the doorway. Several impatient passengers pulled out their carry-ons and began pushing their way toward the exit.

We had reached our destination—a narrow circle of white sand in the middle of nowhere, populated by several hundred settlers living in tin shacks. Every thirty seconds waves three feet high lashed the deserted, sparkling beach. I had to conclude that only someone with a death wish would wade out into the open sea on West Island; I'd packed my bathing suit in vain.

As I was getting off the plane, the copilot opened up the luggage compartment next to me. Two Chinese men in boiler suits walked over and began to hoist the suitcases onto the tarmac. A morbidly obese white man started yelling at them; they had probably been too rough with his luggage.

I must admit I'd been expecting a welcoming committee, or at least a driver. But as there was nowhere you could go on West Island anyway, and therefore there weren't even any cars, this notion was as pointless as it was absurd. When the last passengers trickled into the neighboring settlement, chitchatting along the way, I tried to figure out what to do next.

The airport was surrounded by swaying palm trees. There was just one road. Since nowhere on the atoll was asphalted beyond the airstrip, I had to drag my suitcase through the sand. To the left, turquoise breakers crashed onto the beach. The sound was drowned out by the plane's engines roaring back into life. I looked around and watched as the plane taxied and lifted off. The sky was so clear that minutes later I could still make out the small dot on the horizon. When it finally disappeared, the last link that connected me to the outside world was severed. I told myself the next plane would come along soon enough; after all, the island had to get its supplies from somewhere. So everything was fine for the time being—the way back home wasn't permanently cut off to me.

Feeling reassured by this thought, and having nothing better to do, I headed toward the settlement. The road was strewn with cracked-open coconuts that emitted a stench like rotten egg whites. After about three minutes a stocky man with pigment spots on his face came toward me, gesticulating helplessly and giving me a guilty look. His demeanor suggested he was some form of public official.

"I'm Charly, the mayor of West Island. Forgive me—I was unable to pick you up as planned. I had a prior engagement. I do apologize. Anyway, I've found you now."

"Don't worry," I said.

Then he added, in the authoritative tone of an official notification, that an object had been left for me. He beckoned me into a corrugated tin shack, where I was greeted by the sight of a broken neon sign displaying the Heineken logo and a considerable array of liquor bottles. Maybe drinking was all there was to do in this godforsaken place. In addition to his office as mayor of the island, it turned out that Charly was also its bartender.

"Can I pour you a drink?"

"Whiskey on the rocks."

As I was sipping my scotch, he went over to a locker and opened it with a small key. A full bodysuit made from thick orange-red rubber hung inside it. The mayor wrestled the monstrosity, which had sewed-on boots, out of the locker and draped it over the bar next to me. The unwieldy immersion suit—that's what it was—had to weigh at least thirty pounds.

He politely ignored my blank stare.

"Someone who was on the flight before yours dropped this off here. I'll show you where you can put it on. You still have another couple of hours."

After the sun had set, Charly took me to the tip of a narrow peninsula. He told me I was to put on the suit and wait there—that was all he could tell me; he knew nothing more. After an awkward goodbye, he left me to my task.

Behind me, waves were lapping the white seam of the lagoon, while in front of me, breakers over six feet high crashed onto the beach. Some fifty yards ahead a giant howitzer—a relic from World War Two—stood in the water, rusting away. The barrel was bent and pointed down at the foam that was frothing around the piece of artillery. From my angle looking down onto the cannon, it looked like the broken wing of an ancient bird. The air was humid and it was still sweltering. Thankfully a slight breeze had picked up, stirring the canopy of palm leaves above my head. I let some fine sand run through my fingers.

I started trying to squeeze myself into the orange neoprene safety gear with all my clothes still on. As I was trying to get my left arm into the narrow sleeve, I caught sight of a green navigation light out at sea. I peered into the darkness and made out two other cones of light above the crest of a wave. While the green light was stationary, the other two were rapidly getting closer.

Out of the darkness, a long, thin ship's tender appeared, speeding toward the broken howitzer. I grabbed the zipper and pulled it up to my chin. A figure dressed in an immersion suit like mine jumped from the vessel and tied it to the cannon's crank. A second figure waved at me with a flashlight. I understood the instruction and waded out into the sea. Immediately, I felt the pull of the current. I only just managed to keep my balance. In the distance I saw a wave some thirteen feet high rolling toward me. I had fifteen seconds at best to get over to the speedboat. My right foot sank deep into the soft sand. I stumbled. The man who had tied up the tender came running toward me in his heavy getup. He dragged me over toward the boat, swept me up into a fireman's lift and deposited me inside the vessel. Then he came lumbering after me with the untied rope. The captain pushed the throttle all the way down, and the vessel lurched away from the beach with a jolt and rode up over the first wave before it could break.

In the trough that followed, the bow suddenly twisted to the other side. I hadn't been paying attention and was hurled violently against the onboard storage locker. Two arms helped me into a bucket seat and fastened a harness belt over my chest. We skewed from one wave to the next; we were thrown up into the air and flooded with water. The powerful engine pushed us on through the choppy brine. The propeller churned up the water behind us so violently that millions of glittering air bubbles rose up to the surface.

It wasn't long before we came upon the ship from which the tender had come, outlined against the starry sky like a paper cutout. The shape I could make out was not unlike a dhow, except more futuristic and without the characteristic sail. We swung alongside the ship in a fast, circular motion. Two gripper arms came down, grabbed onto our railing, and lifted us clean out of the surging sea. After the metal claws dropped us into a recess in the side of the hull, one of my escorts indicated that it was safe to step out. There were two people waiting for me by an open door in the bulkhead. On the left was a steward in a white uniform, whose thinning hair had been carefully combed over his bald patch. He helped me peel off my dry suit. Next to him a stocky man in shorts was standing, waiting. He was about sixty and had a friendly face that reminded me of Edward G. Robinson, with clever little eyes. If we'd been in Berlin, I would have taken him for the owner of a corner store.

"Welcome on board the *Dolphin*, Beatrice," he said.

I thought for a moment.

"You're N—!"

He flashed me a broad grin with a sardonic tinge.

"You don't miss anything, do you?"

He showed me the way into the hold of the ship. With their mir-

rors, oversized porcelain vases and brasswork polished to a dazzling shine, the corridors reminded me of the hallways in luxury
hotels. Before I could take further exception to the showy Dubai
chic of the interior design, we took an elevator up onto the bridge.
There was a large digital-chart table in the center which was illuminated from below. I looked out through the huge windshield down
onto the deck. A helicopter was parked there; it looked like a fat
insect. The situation seemed increasingly surreal to me.

N— beckoned over the steward. "Would you like to have some
dinner?"

"No thank you," I replied politely. "I'm jet lagged and I don't
have much of an appetite. But I'd love a coffee, black, no sugar."

"You're quite the spartan, aren't you?"

"I have other priorities right now, that's all," I replied.

N— seemed to like that answer.

"We're quite similar, you and I, even if it may not look that way
at first glance," he said.

"I suspect you're a more baroque personality than I am," I countered cheekily.

"You mean because of the decor? That's just to intimidate business partners."

As he got up from his chair, I was handed a cup of coffee. I took
a sip. N— surveyed me from head to toe.

"You take your coffee black and you don't wear any jewelry—
not even a wedding ring. Married to your work, are you?"

I bristled slightly at his comment. He beamed at me in response.
He had a brusque charm that he could turn on and off at will. The
sharp retort I'd been about to fire back in response to his provoca-
tion died on my lips.

"Oh, now I've offended you," he said. "Before I get myself into
any more trouble, I'd better show you why I've invited you here."

He gestured for me to follow him. As we walked to the stairs, I
noticed that the crew members we passed turned away from us. I

learned later that his employees were under strict instructions to turn their faces to the wall in his presence. Whether this was for reasons of security or just to humiliate his subordinates I never found out.

We took the elevator deep down below the waterline, to where the engine room was. To our right, the generator that supplied the ship with electricity was blinking away. N— took me to a locked door with a camera mounted on it. He looked straight into the lens, and the door opened of its own accord. He gave me a pleased look.

"That's a biometric system," he explained. "It only opens if it recognizes my face. I'm sure you know that every face is unique."

"Of course. They have that stuff at every airport nowadays, don't they? Every passport photo is biometric," I replied.

"So I'm not telling you anything new! You're right, it's like at passport control— the device scans my face and identifies me based on its measurements and proportions. That's one way of using biometrics. But there are others too."

He politely let me go ahead of him. When I entered the space that opened up behind the door, the sight knocked the breath out of me. I had expected another room, but this was a long hall that stretched over half the length of the yacht. Six-feet-tall black boxes were lined up in long rows. Their fronts were covered in small light-emitting diodes. Together the dark columns, connected by cables, made up the biggest server farm I'd ever seen.

"Pretty, isn't it?" N— said with the satisfaction of a villain from a James Bond movie who has built an especially diabolical machine to bring about world destruction.

"Well, pretty is relative," I replied drily, keeping a neutral facial expression.

He ignored my understated reaction.

"What you're seeing here is ninety-nine hundred teraflops, a machine capable of billions of computations per second. It's an IBM

Blue Gene. There are only four supercomputers in the world more powerful than this. We installed it here on the *Dolphin* so that it can be cooled with seawater. My ship just got back from Antarctica, where the computer was running at full capacity. We shut it down a week ago. With warm tropical water in the cooling system it would catch fire within ten minutes."

"And why do you need all this computing power?" I asked.

"Aaaah!" he said, drawing out the vowel. "You're asking all the right questions, Beatrice."

He led me around the long corridors and looked up at the rectangular behemoths like a proud father.

"The answer," he said solemnly, "is biometry. We've fed billions of pictures of people that we sourced online into it—from Facebook profiles, Flickr, Instagram, and so on. The Blue Gene compares the biometric data of the person in the photograph with a second database which is full of portraits from the early days of photography. The computer looks for matches between the biometric data of these deceased people and of those who are currently alive."

I looked at him in wonder, not least because I couldn't see what use there could be in this kind of procedure. "Since every face exists only once, there shouldn't be any matches. So why go through all this effort?" I asked.

He gave me a surprised look, as if I'd said something unbelievably profound.

"Yes, people told me not to get my hopes up—you're really very sharp. And you're absolutely right: no set of biometric data should exist twice. Unless, that is, the person in the picture is someone who is both—alive *and* dead. In almost every culture in the world there is a word for this kind of being. We call it a *revenant*; it's called a *draugr* in Iceland, a *neamh-mairbh* in Ireland, a *Nachzehrer* in Switzerland, a *nosferatù* in Transylvania. We're looking for concrete evidence of their existence. And finally we've been successful—after one sextillion biometric comparisons, our computer has found a match. A person was photographed in 1901 who can also be seen in a picture from 2015, not having aged in the slightest. A revenant, in other words."

"Could it be a mistake?"

"No, we compared the two pictures using the latest biometric methods. It's one and the same person."

In my work—market research—I've learned to pick up on participants' every movement. Sometimes you can tell that someone is lying from tiny things—a brief flutter of the eyes, a fleeting gesture, a tapping foot.

N— was completely relaxed as he looked at me.

He pulled out his cell phone and showed me a sepia-tone oval studio photograph that had the typical charm of the fin-de-siècle. It showed a middle-aged man with a thin mustache wearing a wing-collar shirt. His face looked a little crumpled—not unlike a certain breed of dog whose name escapes me right now.

N— swiped the screen with his index finger, and a new photo appeared. The digital snapshot showed a small group of people sitting at a table that had been set and decorated for Christmas. The decor looked like that of a more upscale chain hotel, complete with the sort of meal you might expect—one step up from a TV dinner. A buxom woman in a blouse and leather skirt was looking into the camera, slightly tipsy. Somewhat off to the side, a party guest who seemed melancholy was pouring punch into a tea glass. I saw immediately that this man and the other from the turn of the century looked uncannily similar.

"His name is Bruno Plischke," N— said. "At least that's what he calls himself. This is a picture we found on Pinterest from an employee Christmas party. Until several months ago he was working at Berlin Brandenburg Airport, but he has recently disappeared. I want you to find Plischke and interrogate him."

"About what?"

"We need further indications as to his identity. We searched the archives for information about the person he used to be, but we didn't turn up anything. I just want to know more, do you understand? Knowledge for knowledge's sake."

"Why did you pick me? Isn't this a job for a private detective?"

"My most trusted right-hand man, Laske, thinks very highly of you. And we need someone with your profile."

He casually handed me a folded-up copy of a Berlin tabloid. "If you want to know more, read this. I also advise you to contact the director of human resources for Berlin Brandenburg Airport, a man by the name of Reinhardt Schneider. Calling him an airport veteran would be an understatement. He's a dinosaur now, long overdue for retirement. The job he's got right now is kind of absurd—hiring people for an airport that'll likely never open. He was the one to hire Plischke."

With the briefest of gestures, N— ended the tour of his inner sanctum. He wasted neither time nor words; perhaps that's what had enabled him to get so rich. That same night his helicopter left the *Dolphin* for Jakarta. As I watched him go, I thought to myself that he had the combination of greatness and hubris that you only find in visionaries.

Many hours of traveling later, I was back in my apartment in Berlin. I looked out the window onto the firewall of the building next door. Several pigeons were perched on top of it. After some time, for no discernible reason, they rose and flew off into the uniformly gray Berlin sky.

I opened the magazine that N— had given me. Somewhere in the middle an article had been marked with a cross. It was about some nutjob who was harassing women in the Wrangelkiez neighborhood. He wasn't a rapist—he was a crazy man who would ambush his victims and jump onto their backs from behind. It seemed he specifically targeted athletic women in their middle years. Apart from the shock no one had actually been hurt. After his strange behavior, the man would flee as suddenly as he had appeared. The police were on the lookout for the stranger, but so far they were coming up empty-handed.

I wondered why N— was interested in this case. Maybe he thought the perpetrator might be Bruno Plischke? I was struck by the unpleasant thought that N— might be using me as a decoy—I did, after all, match the description of the victims.

For a moment I considered washing my hands of the whole affair, but then I thought better of it. The guy in the article sounded like a harmless nutcase—I wasn't afraid of people like that. Eventually I rummaged around in my desk drawer, pulled out the pepper spray that I had bought some time back, and threw it into my purse.

I then began to systematically go about the task N— had set me. I started by calling the management company charged with overseeing the construction of Berlin Brandenburg Airport, and letting them put me through to Schneider's office. He wasn't in, so I left a message with his assistant. About an hour later, she called me back to tell me that Herr Schneider would like to meet me for lunch at the airport the following day.

"But the airport isn't open yet," I said.

"There's a skeleton crew here," she replied. "Someone will let you in."

I almost missed the appointment, so jammed up with traffic was the A-10, the Autobahn that circles the city. After a while, Berlin Brandenburg Airport appeared on the horizon: a huge glass-fronted galleria with departure gates built in front of it, clearly botched before it had left the drawing board; a palatial eyesore that had been under construction for the past fifteen years. Once hyped as Berlin's "futuristic" airport, the project suffered from the conflicting ambitions of its architect, Meinhard von Gerkan, and the director of the management company, Rainer Schwarz. Even the name had been the subject of dithering and debate—Berlin Brandenburg or Willy Brandt. Somewhat ironic for a project founded on the spirit of German unity, and so embarrassingly at odds with the idea of German efficiency that even American magazines had taken to cackling at it.

And yet this faltering enterprise was in many ways symptomatic of the times. It seemed every airport in Berlin was a reflection of its era. Just across the airfield was the old East German airport, Schönefeld, built by a system that recognized travel was an expression of freedom and sought to discourage its citizens from it with repellent architecture. The utilitarian West German architecture of Tegel strove only to promote efficient time management; the recently shuttered Tempelhof had been erected to convince the arriving visitors of the glory of the Third Reich. Berlin was a playground full of ideologues with trowels, who would build palaces for the people and then tear them down again only to erect new monstrosities on the still-fresh ruins.

Now, with free-market capitalism trying to get a stranglehold on Berlin, the latest incarnation of this pattern was a maze of stores with the boarding gates tacked on somewhere behind.

I took the Brandenburg exit and, after passing through a security barrier, followed the directions I had been given and found my way to the company's headquarters, several nondescript buildings set between terminals A and B. I was made to wait for Herr Schneider, who came down from his office and asked, by way of greeting, whether I was hungry. After a handshake, he led me off toward the food court. The restaurants were all closed, of course, but a makeshift buffet had been laid out for the airport's employees. I graced my plate with a Wiener schnitzel that had been fried to within an inch of its life. I didn't help myself to any of the side salad; it looked even more unsavory than the main dish. Schneider decided on the salmon—

probably in an attempt to demonstrate that he was not afraid of fish poisoning as, after twenty years in public service, he was immune to all bacteria.

He was a long, thin man with the fingers of a pianist.

"If I understand correctly, you are interested in an administrative position. There's not a whole lot up for grabs in that department right now," he began, rummaging around at length in his papers.

"Actually things aren't quite the way I told you."

Schneider looked up from his food and eyed me mistrustfully through his thick glasses.

"How do you mean?" he asked sharply.

"It's about a strictly confidential matter, that's why I couldn't be entirely open with your assistant. I'm not looking for a job at all—I work for the Federal Office for Information Security. One of your former colleagues applied for a position with us, but we're not sure whether he's a suitable candidate."

"And so you came to me under false pretenses?"

"Please understand my position—from one HR professional to another. We are involved in top-secret projects—we work with the Federal Criminal Police Office among others. I couldn't use the official route in such a delicate matter."

Schneider wiped his mouth with a napkin.

"This is highly unusual," he said reproachfully.

"It's about a man by the name of Bruno Plischke."

Schneider looked at me, aghast.

"What, Plischke, our company mailman? We fired him three weeks ago—I wouldn't touch him if I were you."

"Why? Did he harass any women?"

Schneider gave me a disturbed look.

"Of course not!" he said irritably.

"And where can I find Plischke now?"

"I thought he applied for a job with you?"

"Yes, but then he disappeared. That's exactly what's so strange."

"I have no idea. One colleague said she saw him at the drop-in center at the mission inside Ostbahnhof train station. That's all I know. Listen, this is all most unusual. Please tell your boss to submit a formal request."

"Of course," I said, flashing my most charming smile and wrapping my silk shawl around my neck. I took a coaster and wrote down my number.

"If you think of anything else about Mr. Plischke, why don't you give me a call."

Schneider took the coaster between finger and thumb as if it were a used handkerchief.

I took the S-Bahn to Neukölln station and changed to the circle line. The train was completely packed—apparently several earlier trains had been canceled. I squeezed in between an elegantly dressed African woman and a rake-thin girl who had a raven's head tattooed onto the back of her hand.

At Ostbahnhof I walked down the stairs toward the concourse at the front of the station that faced onto the Strasse der Pariser Kommune and the brick postal-service building. A small group of homeless people were standing in the arcade to my right. Two of them had dogs with them that were extensively sniffing each other. When the animals had finished establishing contact, one of them—a mangy cross between a Münsterländer and a Bracco Italiano—barked, inviting play. The other dog ignored him, however, snuffling at a cigarette butt instead.

The barker's owner was an aging punk with a bleach-blond mohawk. Just twenty years before, squatters and punks had been a fixture in the cityscape, but now they were a dying breed, gawked at and photographed by tourists. Only when they were among themselves, like right now, could they forget the fact that their way of life had become an anachronism when the old Federal Republic had ceased to exist. They washed up at the mission like flotsam, intermingling with other latecomers and outsiders.

I walked into the sparse reception area of the shelter and looked around. Visitors were sitting at several of the tables, drinking tea and warming up. One of the chairs was occupied by a startlingly thin woman who was staring glassy-eyed at the floor. She seemed aware of neither the outside world nor her own body, which at this point was barely serviceable as the vessel for her life force anymore. She probably had a drug problem or was suffering from tuberculosis. I was hit by the realization that I lived in a parallel world. As I whiled away my time on luxury yachts and in swanky office buildings, other people in this city were fighting for their very lives.

I crossed the room and took one of the leaflets that were stacked up on a stool. I was cold, so I sat down by the radiator. A consultation was going on at the table next to me. I glanced over surreptitiously at the two people. On the left was a young Syrian man in a white bomber jacket, nervously playing with his phone. A woman had sat down next to him and seemed to be trying to talk him down. She was about fifty, and had red-framed glasses and braces to correct her crooked incisors. I was struck by her pleasant, melodious voice.

In the middle of the conversation she looked over at me. Her gaze was neither curious nor appraising—just a first attempt to reach out from one person to another.

After some time, the lady with the braces came up to my table.

"Hi, I'm Ingrid."

"Beatrice."

"Would you like a drink? Tea, perhaps?'

"If it's not too much trouble."

"Of course not, that's why I'm here."

As she walked over to a tall counter to boil the water in an electric kettle, I silently prepared myself for the fact that I would be lying to this woman. Normally I don't have a problem with that if it serves the cause. Call me cynical if you want—I think it's pragmatic. You need to cut some corners if you want to get anywhere in this life.

But right then I felt conflicted. It occurred to me that Ingrid probably did her work here on a voluntary basis.

"Are you looking to get involved, or do you want to talk?" she asked gently.

"Neither. I'm looking for someone."

"I understand."

Without my having asked her, she handed me a small jug of milk and some sugar.

"Are you looking for your child?"

"No, for a man."

She nodded sympathetically.

"You're worried. Have you already been to the police?"

"No," I replied. "And I don't want to. It's not my husband I'm looking for—it's an acquaintance."

Ingrid rose up onto her elbows and leaned a little closer to signal that I could count on her attention and discretion.

"When did he disappear?"

"About two weeks ago. I work at the airport. He had a job there as a courier. But he suddenly got fired. I always liked him, even if he was a bit rough around the edges. I don't want him to suffer! A colleague recently saw him here. I'd like to find him and help him. We collected money for him in the office."

"Do you have any idea why he took off?"

"I'm afraid he fell into a depression after he lost his job. He was always rather melancholy."

I pulled out my phone and opened up the picture of the Christmas party that N— had shown me on the *Dolphin*. I zoomed in on Plischke's face and held my phone up for Ingrid.

For the first time in our conversation she lost control over her body language. Her patient, understanding expression gave way to bewilderment. A fraction of a second later, she had composed herself again.

"Yes, I know him," she said neutrally.

"Can you tell me where to find him?"

"Probably in Beer Heaven."

I must have looked pretty baffled. Ingrid gave me an apologetic look and added that Beer Heaven was a bar.

"The clientele consists exclusively of alcoholics. All men. This guy . . . your colleague . . . I'd be careful of him if I were you. He got very abusive in here more than once. You know, people change. Alcohol can do terrible things."

That's all she wanted to say about Plischke.

I thanked Ingrid and promised her that I would be careful. As I left the station, I had a queasy feeling in my stomach, but possibly my heavy lunch was to blame.

Beer Heaven faced onto the back of the Böhmischer Gottesacker cemetery, three minutes from Karl-Marx-Strasse U-Bahn station. Here, Neukölln was still Neukölln—not the trendy nightlife district that attracted tourists and artists on Schillerpromenade. The garbagemen seemed to have written off this part of the neighborhood. An indistinct mixture of food scraps, plastic bags, and sanitary towels came wafting out of the trash cans. Someone had shoved a used syringe into a shoebox; it protruded from the cardboard like a poison arrow.

The bar I was looking for was on a corner. Yellowish lace curtains hung in the windows. The joint seemed cut off from the outside world, almost barricaded off—a parallel world for those in the know. A blackboard was propped up in the window listing the drinks that were available: from Berliner Weisse *mit Schuss*—beer with a shot of

Waldmeister liqueur on the side—to more exotic combinations with names like *square*, *tower ghost*, and *mouse piss*. Above the door was a frosted-glass sign, lit up inside with energy-saving bulbs, that bore the name of the establishment in burgundy Gothic script.

When I entered, I was hit by the smell of stale cigarette smoke and vomit. Several figures were sitting hunched over at the bar. Schmaltzy *Schlager* songs—Freddy Quinn's greatest hits—were coming out of a crackling speaker. A woman whose face was caked with lurid makeup was standing behind the bar pouring the guests a round of cheap Korn liqueur.

"This one's on Olli," she said.

The men mumbled a thank-you in the direction of a guy in his late sixties dressed in threadbare heavy-metal clothes. He let out a small burp, but otherwise gave off an air of complete apathy.

I looked around. Right next to him I spotted the person I was looking for. Bruno Plischke was more compact than I had imagined him—five feet six inches at most—but very muscular. He sat there, his legs spread wide, and knocked back the Korn in one gulp. Then he ran a large hand through his hair. He seemed restless, his face flushed, like someone with high blood pressure. When the door banged shut he turned around to face me, so that I could see his bulldog-like facial features in the half-light. Involuntarily, a shiver ran down my spine.

The other guests also looked over at me through the smoke-thick air. I found myself gazing into five pairs of bloodshot eyes; Plischke's were the reddest.

The man named Olli pointed at me with a toothpick.

"Look, the chicken's run home to roost," he slurred.

"It's *come* home, not run. Come, as in: when I lay on top of her, I *came*!" one of his drinking buddies corrected him from the other end of the bar.

"Leave her alone, guys," the woman behind the bar admonished.

"Whiskey on the rocks," I said and sat down next to Plischke, carefully hanging my purse off the bar stool so I'd have my pepper spray within reach.

Once the glass was in front of me, I saw out of the corner of my eye that Plischke was staring at my drink.

"Would you like one too? It's on me," I asked without looking directly at him.

He growled something inaudible.

"Another one for the gentleman."

The bartender frowned, but followed my instructions. Before Plischke had touched it, I clinked my glass against his.

"Cheers. You look familiar somehow. I work at Berlin Brandenburg Airport."

Plischke's eyes flashed. He pulled the drink over toward him and drank it in one swig.

"Next time no ice, eh?" he said gruffly.

"Did I see you there at some point? They're a funny bunch over there. I don't like my job very much. The people from the operating company aren't fair to me."

I sipped my whiskey and hoped that Plischke would take the bait.

"They're crooks," he spat out. His face contorted into a hateful grimace.

"I wish I could find another job," I continued as if I hadn't heard his sudden outburst. "But what am I supposed to do? I can't be cabin crew—I'm afraid of flying."

Plischke's facial features relaxed. He let the ice cubes clink together in his empty glass.

"And how does this fear express itself?" he asked.

"Palpitations, panic attacks, nausea, dizziness."

"But the new planes are so safe. They're nothing like they used to be."

"What were they like before?"

"I crashed five times. Survived them all."

I gaped at him.

"Are you a pilot?"

"I used to be."

Plischke fell silent. I should have left him alone. But he'd piqued my curiosity, so I pressed ahead.

"Tell me about the crashes."

"That was at the old airport," he said brusquely.

"Tempelhof?"

"No, the *old* airport, not any of those new ones. Look, I don't know what you want from me."

Plischke pushed away the empty glass. He seemed upset. His brow furrowed like a contracted accordion. He pulled a crumpled five-euro bill from his pants pocket and threw it onto the bar. He put on his jacket and got up without paying any further attention to me. When he opened the door, cold wind blew into the cave-like saloon. For a fraction of a second his compact body was outlined in the door opening against the light of the low evening sun. When I made to go after him, he had already disappeared. A soft murmur passed along the row of drinkers, but then the men sank back into their beer fug.

After this meeting, Plischke vanished without a trace. I made some inquiries, but neither the bartender nor the neighbors in the rental houses on the block knew where he lived, if he even had an apartment, or whether he was employed anywhere. Hardly anyone remembered him, and if they did, they only described vague, shadowy impressions. But since our brief meeting Plischke was no longer a phantom to me.

"So you're looking to write an article about the first Berlin airport?"

"That's right. I work for *Die Zeit*."

Dr. Gertrud Schilling was the curator of the Technology Museum's aviation department. She was wiry, with a dyed-blonde bob and three studs in each ear, which completed the impression of an edgy left-wing intellectual.

"Your history page is pretty decent, certainly better than the politics section, anyway," she said.

Dr. Schilling seemed to like me—she winked at me, which was probably her idea of flirting. I smiled back.

On our way to the archive, we passed through a workshop with the hull of an old plane in it, propped up on scaffolding. "A Ju 87. We're building one complete model out of three different wrecks— it's a joint project with the aviation museum in Bodø."

She unlocked a room that smelled like newly laid linoleum and was full of cabinets containing large hanging files. As she opened one of them, she asked me how much I knew about the old airport.

"Nothing, really."

She frowned—I had probably confirmed her worst prejudices about journalism.

"Right," she said sharply. "Let's get to it then."

She opened a drawer and pulled out a stack of black-and-white photos.

"Some of these are also upstairs in the permanent collection," she said.

The first picture showed several haphazardly built wooden shacks at the edge of a field.

"This is Germany's first airport. Berlin-Johannisthal. First went into operation in 1909. All the well-known pioneers flew there: Manfred von Richthofen, Melli Beese, Paul Engelhard . . ."

She put a second picture onto a table in front of me. It had been taken from a similar angle, but now the foreground was full of delicate machines made out of wood and sailcloth. Some of the contraptions resembled swans with outspread wings; others had several different levels of tautly stretched cloth, like Chinese pagodas. They were driven by wooden propellers that had been polished to a shine. It was hard to imagine that these planes could ever have lifted themselves into the air.

Dr. Schilling seemed to have read my mind.

"Aviation was in its infancy. Some models would only fly a few meters; others would flip upside down uncontrollably. People routinely died in these attempts. Every weekend curious onlookers would flock to Johannisthal to see the flights and the crashes. Sometimes the field would be so full of spectators that the pilots had to draw their revolvers and fire warning shots to drive them back off the airstrip. After a crash, people would run up to the burning wrecks and pull out parts to take home as souvenirs. It was like the Wild West."

I showed her my cell phone with the picture of Plischke in the wing-collar shirt.

"Was this man one of the people who flew there?"

Dr. Schilling took my phone and studied the image.

"Hmm. That's Rolf Ott, I believe. One moment . . ."

She pulled out another picture in which two men in leather helmets were posing in front of a white glider that resembled a dandelion puff. The crumpled face of the man on the right was unmistakable.

"This is Ott with Edmund Rumpler, the manufacturer of the Rumpler Taube, a popular model of aircraft from the early years. Ott was Rumpler's test pilot—he was crazy about flying. When the civilian use of Johannisthal came to an end in 1923, he never got over it. Rumpler had to fire him at the time—with immediate effect. Shortly after that Ott disappeared in a stolen sports plane, an Arado SC II."

"What do you mean disappeared?"

"He went missing. He crossed over the Mecklenburg Lakeland and never came back. They never found any wreckage."

✖

After my meeting at the Technology Museum, I wrote N— an elaborate update on where I was at with my research. Soon afterward I got a call from Laske, my contact in Berlin. He asked to meet up with me. We convened at the oyster bar on Gendarmenmarkt as we had the last time. Laske showed up ten minutes late, a thin ostrich-leather folder wedged under his arm.

"Your research was very valuable," he began. "We are sure now that Rolf Ott and Bruno Plischke are one and the same."

"It is crazy how the pieces of the puzzle seem to fit together, isn't it? But if I'm honest, surely it *has* to be a coincidence that they look so much alike, don't you think? After all, there's no such thing as ghosts. I sat next to Plischke—the man is made of flesh and blood, a drunk from Neukölln."

Laske patiently folded his hands in front of his stomach.

"I know this is all a lot for you to process. Your skepticism is completely natural. But our research has brought to light other connections that you should know about before you make up your mind."

He opened the folder and pulled out a flyer that said "Tempelhof Must Remain a Commercial Airport!"

"In 2008, the Christian Democrats launched a campaign against the closure of Tempelhof Airport. Do you remember? Shortly before the referendum there was a huge IT failure in the offices of the group that was lobbying to preserve it. Someone erased all the hard drives overnight. A suspect was arrested almost immediately, but they had to let him go again due to lack of evidence. His name was Bruno Plischke. And that's not all. A year later, a homeless man was caught in the woodland near Tegel Airport cutting through the optic-fiber cable that led to the control tower. He was IDed as Rolf Ott. On the way to the police station the man broke loose, ran off in the direction of Plötzensee lake, and disappeared. A similar incident happened at Schönefeld Airport where a man matching Rolf Ott's description was spotted."

"So you're saying Plischke, or Ott, is sabotaging the airports in Berlin because he is angry that Johannisthal got shut down?"

"Looks that way."

When I pulled up to my apartment building, it was already midnight. As I turned off the car radio, I was still running the strange conversation that I'd had with Laske over in my head.

I stepped out onto the deserted street. There'd been a drizzle earlier; the gray cobblestones were glistening. Suddenly I heard a faint noise—a stone crunching underfoot. In the glass panel of the gas streetlight I spotted a shadow waiting for me in the doorway. I knew who it was immediately.

"You're late," Plischke said.

I nodded dumbly. My hand moved to my side, but I only had my small clutch bag with me, not the big purse with the pepper spray.

His arm glided around my neck like a snake—except snakes aren't that cold. He pulled me close to him, spinning me around counterclockwise and pressing up against me. Through our layers of clothes, I felt his chest against the small of my back, a grid of taut muscle.

He was breathing calmly and regularly, like people do when they're completely sure of themselves. Now the other hand started to feel its way, first grazing my shoulder blade and then moving around to my collarbone. At the same time, Plischke thrust his hips against me from behind, but he was not aroused: his penis was limp.

Casually, as if it were the most natural thing in the world, he jumped onto my back from behind, wrapped his legs—which were dressed in gray pleated pants—around my hips, and crossed his ankles in front of my body. His shoes were battered oxblood brogues that he must have polished recently, because the toe caps were gleaming. The right shoe had a small hole in the tip of the leather sole, just under the toes—it went right through to the insole. He'd probably stepped on a sharp pebble.

We stood like that for a moment—me slightly tilted forward and him riding me piggyback.

"Let's go," he ordered.

Without thinking, I headed towards the Spree River.

Plischke was surprisingly light, or maybe it was just that I was very fit. I go to the gym regularly, work the rowing machine for thirty minutes, and then strengthen my latissimus dorsi against sixty pounds of resistance on the weight stack, which I pull down vertically in front of my chest in three rounds of about fifteen minutes each, followed by thirty-five sit-ups on a yoga mat, straight—that is, without pausing—and to finish I do the Five Tibetans. We progressed with commensurate speed.

After about eight minutes we had reached the East Side Gallery. A drunk Italian man, who had gotten lost on his way to the Watergate club, gaped at us. There were intermittent bursts of traffic coming from Mitte, but none of the cars stopped or even slowed down.

Near the famous graffiti of the Trabant breaking through the Berlin Wall, it suddenly occurred to me that I could just run back, smash Plischke against the concrete, and break his ribs. I was strong enough to violently throw him off. I accelerated to gain momentum, but it was as if he was reading my mind. He dug his elbow in, almost imperceptibly constricting my air supply—a modest, impersonal threat. I immediately slowed my pace, and his arm relaxed again. When we got to the Oberbaum Bridge, for a moment I wasn't sure which way to turn. I decided to stay on our side of the river. At the end of Stralauer Allee I turned north and then circled east, onto Hauptstrasse.

I don't know if it just seemed that way because I'd had Plischke on my back for so long, or whether something strange had already started happening, but he suddenly stopped feeling as light as he had in the beginning. What even *did* he weigh—150 pounds?

My adrenaline levels had come down a little now, and I started to notice details that had escaped me before. For one thing, Plischke's breath, which stank of beer; and I noticed that his legs—which I could see poking out between his socks and pant legs—were uncommonly hairy.

A row of turnkey modern townhouses shaped like cubes appeared before us—each with its own gunmetal Audi parked in front. Every one of these architectural faux pas had found a buyer straightaway.

As I was walking I began to notice I wasn't doing so well. Something was wrong with my pulse—it was even higher than after the uphill workout on the treadmill that I sometimes did. Normally my stamina is very good ("Beatrice has iron lungs," my personal trainer always says) but now I was having to slow my pace considerably.

I thought about how, when you're in the car, you don't notice just how far Köpenicker Chaussee runs along Rummelsburger Bay.

It seemed like an eternity before the imposing heat and power plant loomed up in front of us. Its high smokestacks were snorting out white columns of smoke, up into the darkness. Invisible air currents seized the dragon's breath, tore it away from the chimneys, and scattered it into the night. Above me, a freight car filled with briquettes clattered along a steel overpass. A second load of coal tipped into the glittering furnace with a loud rumbling noise. Plischke seemed impatient; he shifted his weight from right to left and back to the center. It was 1:30 in the morning by now, maybe even later. I tried to walk faster, but I couldn't match the speed that I'd been doing in the beginning. When we got to the old transformer station, I had to stop to catch my breath. I leaned against the crumbling brickwork of the main hall. With its shattered, hollow windows it looked like a cathedral against the night sky. Inside, rats were scurrying around between copper coils and rusting transformers. Progress had moved in here a hundred years ago with great fanfare, only to slip away down the basement stairs into the wild yonder.

Plischke seemed to be losing patience with me; he dug his heels into my stomach. I tried to breathe my way through the pain and started moving again. My burden now seemed twice as heavy as before. A drop of sweat ran down my forehead and onto the bridge of my titanium-steel glasses and remained hanging there.

When we got to Wuhlheide, we crossed over the Spree. A houseboat moored on the other side of the river was rocking gently on the water. About ten swans were gathered in front of it. They had tucked their heads under their wings to sleep and were floating on the dark surface of the river like cotton balls. I stumbled toward a residential neighborhood, but Plischke didn't seem to like that: he grunted and dug his heels in even more. I immediately changed direction, homing in on the S-Bahn tracks instead. I followed along them until I arrived at a community garden.

One of the tenants had sawn out decorative trim under the gable of his shed to make it look like an alpine lodge. A smashed garden gnome was lying on the pebble path next to it. Its hat was so thoroughly pulverized that at first glance it looked like red flour had been ground into the stones with someone's shoe. The next plot of land looked tidier and more orderly. Barbecue tongs hung by the entrance. I was surprised they hadn't been stolen—back in the day, everything that was lying around Berlin unclaimed would be snatched immediately.

Since I was too tired to walk straight, Plischke's behind grazed against the latticework fence that separated the plots of land from each other, sending me reeling. He growled into my ear like an angry dog.

"Easy," I gasped.

Behind the community garden, we entered an open landscape

with a scattering of developments. I suspected that some of these low-rise buildings were part of Adlershof, the former East German radio station—they had the run-down appearance that was typical of this expired state, which had succumbed to neglect with the consent of its citizens.

Plischke weighed at least 170 pounds now. My muscles were screaming—so much lactic acid had built up in them. I touched my head and found to my horror that I was burning up, as though I had a fever. I staggered off toward a field, certain that I was going to die.

Plischke was red with rage. His hands squeezed my breasts until the pain made me see stars. I gathered my last strength and headed toward a high barbed-wire fence. There was an industrial lot behind it. With my right hand I leaned on the fence as I walked, which made it marginally easier to get ahead. At the end of the fence there were other buildings that were part of a sprawling industrial estate.

Gasping for air, I reached the outer perimeter of the estate, which bordered the Groß-Berliner Damm to the south. Right in front of us there was about half a square mile of derelict land. Behind it occasional streetlights were visible, illuminating dreary rowhouses dating back to after the fall of the Wall. Apart from these cold islands of light, it was dark, but my eyes had gotten so used to it by now that I was able to make out a clump of crooked birches, kitty-corner across from us. Right next to it an elevated pedestrian walkway began and then followed all the way around the circumference of the vacant patch of land. With a furious grunting, Plischke drove me toward the walkway. But I was done for. My mouth was parched, and I found myself desperately craving a lemonade with fresh lemon juice, fizzy water, and brown sugar. As I was entertaining this fantasy, a rabbit suddenly came hopping through the grass—not one of those brown city bunnies, but a large buck with its ears standing straight up. I burst into hysterical laughter, swaying to and fro like a leaky canoe. Plischke punched me in the crotch with his right fist. By now I was past caring. I took a run-up and sprinted toward the derelict land that I surmised could only be the former Johannisthal Airport—or rather, its pitiful remains, which had been repurposed into a soulless recreation area. No sooner had I gotten up onto the walkway than I fell headfirst onto the wooden boards. I tasted blood in my mouth; excruciating pain shot through the left side of my face. The last thing I noticed before everything turned black was Plischke jumping off me like a cowboy off a horse that he's ridden to death. With a single leap he sprang down onto the scraggly grass and ran off into the distance, hopping and zig-zagging wildly. When he reached the center of the airfield he disappeared, as if the ground had swallowed him up. After that I saw and heard nothing more.

A jogger found me early the next morning and I was taken in an ambulance to the hospital in Marzahn. The doctors rebuilt my cheekbone with a minimally invasive procedure: they made an incision just under my eye and inserted a tiny plate that pinned the pieces of broken bone back together. My state of exhaustion was treated with various intravenous nutritional supplements. I had temporary crowns fitted in place of the broken-off incisors.

Shortly before they sent me home from the hospital, there was a knock on the door of my room. Laske came in, carrying a huge bouquet of flowers.

"How are you doing?" he asked sheepishly.

"What do you want from me?"

"I understand you are angry with us. We didn't know how dangerous he was."

"You hung me out to dry!"

"Listen, I'm sending you the bonus now, and another fifty thousand as compensation. And I'll email you something tomorrow that will explain the incident."

"You son of a bitch," I choked out.

He put the flowers down on the dresser, shrugged helplessly, and left my room, mumbling an only half-audible apology.

The next day, there was an email from Laske in my inbox that contained a link. I propped myself up onto my pillow, clicked it, and was taken to a Wikipedia article.

The text read:

In mythology, the aufhocker *(Low German:* huckup; *Sorbian:* buback) *is a pressing demon, like a kobold, that jumps onto the shoulders or backs of travelers who are still on the road at night, and becomes heavier with every step. Often the nightmarish visitation happens in two stages. First the traveler will be approached or joined on the road by a sinister being; then it leaps onto the person's back and demands to be carried to the nearest cemetery or some other similarly forbidding location. It is as if the traveler is paralyzed—they suffer from shortness of breath and are incapable of turning around. Some aufhockers let themselves be carried until the victim dies. The oldest reports of aufhockers refer to them as "the leaping dead."*

One week after I was discharged from the hospital my cell phone rang. I had plugged it into the socket next to the bed to charge. I pressed the green button.

"Hello?"

"Hello, this is Schneider from Berlin Brandenburg airport operations."

"Yes?" I asked weakly into the phone.

"I'm calling about this Plischke," Schneider said. "My manager has given me permission to share with you the reason that he got fired. I do hope you didn't hire him?"

"No, we didn't," I replied with effort.

"So, as you might know, we had some problems with the fire safety system at the new airport."

"Yeah, I heard about that."

"Well, it turned out that something was going awry within the company. Construction plans that had been drawn up by our contracting partners were circulating around the office. But by the time they reached the construction managers, they had changed."

"What do you mean?" I asked, confused.

"The technical drawings had been *altered*. Somehow, when they were en route from one department to the other via the interoffice mail, someone falsified them—deliberately drawing mistakes in. And this someone could only have been your Mr. Plischke, our company mailman. I warn you again—this man's shenanigans caused billions of euros worth of damage."

"One bad apple, I guess," I said.

"Isn't that the truth. Have a nice day."

With a little click, Schneider hung up.

ACKNOWLEDGMENTS

THE AUTHOR would like to thank Rebecca Egeling, Wolfgang Hörner, Martje Herzog, Marina Petsalis-Diomidis, Henning Brümmer, Emma Rault, Michael Barron, and the team at Melville House.

ABOUT THE AUTHOR

RUDOLPH HERZOG is an award-winning director, producer, and writer. His BBC/ARD documentary on humor in the Third Reich sold internationally and his book *Dead Funny* on the same subject was named a book of the year by *The Atlantic* in 2012. His second book, the critically acclaimed *Short History of Nuclear Folly*, was published in the U.K., the United States, and Canada. A documentary by Rudolph Herzog based on the book was featured on Arte and Netflix. He has helmed additional documentaries that include a National Geographic special on polar explorer Roald Amundsen and a special on Stasi spy Werner Stiller (*The Agent*). Rudolph is currently expanding into fiction with his feature film *How to Fake a War*, ready for release. Rudolph also co-scripted and executive produced *The White Diamond*, voted Film of the Year by *Time*. Other credits include *The Heist*, a three-part series for Channel 4 (U.K.) in which real criminal masterminds attempt to commit the perfect crime. Rudolph series produced Pro7's 40x40 minute flagship *Galileo Mystery*, as well as *Lefloid Vs. the World* for Google Originals. He lectured at the German Film Academy (DFFB) and worked as an on-staff columnist for *Newsweek*.